"I don't think (anymore," he (

Mariela gave a little half smile as he met her gaze. "I'm glad you don't."

She was too much to resist. He cupped her cheek and leaned forward until their lips were barely an inch apart. "Are you sure?"

"I am," Mariela said and closed the distance between them.

His lips were warm, soft at first, but as the kiss intensified, they became harder. More insistent. And something about the force of it sent a shiver of fear through her.

Sensing it, Ricky tempered his kiss and inched away, but he stroked his thumb across her cheek and then down across her lips. "I would never hurt you."

"I know, it's just... I know," she repeated, reminding herself that Ricky was nothing like her ex. He was thoughtful and caring. The kind of man a woman would want at her side as a partner.

But she'd sensed he had his demons as well.

BRICKELL AVENUE AMBUSH

New York Times Bestselling Author
CARIDAD PIÑEIRO

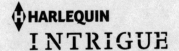

Thank you to all my amazing friends at Liberty States Fiction
Writers for their support and friendship. It's a pleasure to be
able to attend workshops with you and share the trials and
tribulations of being a writer, as well as the successes!

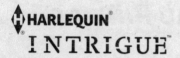

HARLEQUIN®
INTRIGUE™

Recycling programs
for this product may
not exist in your area.

ISBN-13: 978-1-335-58315-4

Brickell Avenue Ambush

Copyright © 2022 by Caridad Piñeiro Scordato

Harlequin Enterprises ULC
22 Adelaide St. West, 41st Floor
Toronto, Ontario M5H 4E3, Canada
www.Harlequin.com

Printed in U.S.A.

New York Times and *USA TODAY* bestselling author **Caridad Piñeiro** is a Jersey girl who just wants to write and is the author of nearly fifty novels and novellas. She loves romance novels, superheroes, TV and cooking. For more information on Caridad and her dark, sexy romantic suspense and paranormal romances, please visit www.caridad.com.

Books by Caridad Piñeiro

Harlequin Intrigue

South Beach Security

Lost in Little Havana
Brickell Avenue Ambush

Cold Case Reopened
Trapping a Terrorist
Decoy Training

Visit the Author Profile page at Harlequin.com.

CAST OF CHARACTERS

Ricardo Gonzalez (Ricky)—A trained psychologist, Ricky helps South Beach Security with their domestic abuse cases and other kinds of civil assignments. When he's not working at the agency, Ricky runs a support group for individuals suffering from trauma.

Mariela Hernandez—Mariela escaped an abusive marriage and is finally reaching for the life she wants after dropping out of college to marry and support her ex-husband.

Ramon Gonzalez III (Trey)—Marine Trey Gonzalez served Miami Beach as an undercover detective before retiring and joining South Beach Security. Trey is the heir apparent to run South Beach Security.

Mia and Carolina Gonzalez—Trey's younger sister Mia and cousin Carolina run a successful lifestyle and gossip blog and are invited to every important event in Miami. That lets "the Twins" gather a lot of information about what is happening in Miami to help South Beach Security with their various investigations.

Josefina (Sophie) and Robert Whitaker Jr.—Trey's cousins Josefina and Robert are genius tech gurus who work at South Beach Security and help the agency with their various investigations.

Chapter One

The executive's chair suited him well, Ricardo Gonzalez thought as his older brother, Trey, sat at the large wooden partner's desk. The built-ins behind the desk were empty, their content in boxes waiting to be unpacked and displayed on the shelves.

"The suit looks good on you, *mano*," he teased, aware that Trey usually reserved suits and ties for special occasions and funerals. That he was uncomfortable was evidenced by the way Trey slipped a finger beneath the collar of his shirt and tugged as if it was too tight.

"*Caray*, Ricky. When I said I'd join the agency, I didn't realize it meant signing up for this every day," Trey said and jerked at the collar again. He pulled open several drawers as if to check what was in them and where he might put his things.

Ricky laughed and sat on the edge of the desk. "You could always try to convince *papi* to go business casual."

Trey playfully pointed in his direction. "Now that sounds like a plan."

A plan. He wasn't sure his brother had a plan given his rather abrupt decision to join South Beach Security after years of fighting his family's wishes that he do so. But maybe nearly getting killed on his last assignment and finding the love of his life was reason enough. However, Ricky still worried about his brother's decision.

"You're sure you want to do this?" he asked, hoping Trey would be happy with his choice.

Trey narrowed his gaze, his aqua-colored eyes assessing. "Trying to psychoanalyze me, *hermanito*? I'm not one of your patients."

He wasn't, but that didn't mean that Ricky couldn't try to take care of him the way he helped his patients. After all, his brother had been through a traumatic experience recently and could possibly use his expertise.

"I know, but I'm here if you ever want to talk or need my help," he said.

Trey chuckled and shook his head. "You know what I could use help with?"

"What?" Ricky said with a smile.

Trey stood and gestured with his fingers in the direction of boxes and built-ins. "You can help me unpack."

"With pleasure," Ricky said and walked over to one of the containers. He hefted the heavy carton onto the wide ledge of the built-in and it landed with a loud thud from the weight of the contents.

"What do you have in here? Rocks?" he teased.

Trey laughed and shook his head. "Books. You more than most should appreciate that."

Ricky tilted his head in agreement. His older brother had always been an all-action guy while as the youngest he'd been the more studious type. Middle sister, Mia, and their cousin Carolina were the social butterflies in the family, which suited their roles as some of Miami's top social media influencers.

"I do appreciate that," Ricky said as he ripped open the box and emptied the assorted books onto the ledge. There were tomes on cybersecurity, forensic investigations, criminal and civil procedure and insurance fraud, as well as several on military history. No surprise on the latter since all the Gonzalez men, except for him, had served as marines.

While he loaded them onto one of the lower shelves in size, order, symmetry and balance—things Ricky needed in his life—he said, "How are the wedding plans going?"

Trey blew out a rough laugh as he unpacked yet more books from a carton. "Roni, her parents and *mami* are busy planning it like generals directing a military campaign."

Ricky glanced at his brother from the corner of his eye. "Maybe because no one ever expected you to finally settle down. Especially with Roni."

His brother paused his unpacking and a wistful smile slipped over his features. His blue-green gaze glittered with happiness. "Roni," he said with a loving sigh. "I can't believe I was so dense that I didn't see it. Didn't see *her* for so long."

But maybe Trey had seen her now because of the recent death and destruction in his life, which again made Ricky worry if it wasn't all too sudden. "She was always there, Trey. Why now?"

Trey plopped a book onto a shelf and faced him, arms across his broad chest. "Asking as my brother or are you in psychologist mode again?"

It was often hard to shut off his profession from the personal, as much as he tried. "Both, Trey," he finally admitted.

His brother stared at him for a long time, his gaze intense, before he said, "I can't deny it's sudden. But I know in here…" He stopped to tap at a spot above his heart. "I know it's the real thing. She makes me feel like no one ever did before."

Trey's words and their tone were so heartfelt any worries Ricky might have had dissipated like the steam coming off a hot Miami pavement after a summer rain. But they also roused an unwanted emotion in him. He wouldn't call it jealousy. Or loneliness. He didn't know what he'd call it; only as happy as he was for his brother, he was…unsure about his own life.

Ricky had been busy building his practice and support group, as well as helping his family at

South Beach Security on occasion. It hadn't left much time for a personal life.

If his very alpha and extreme action brother could come around, he could definitely think about doing something different. Normally he didn't do different but maybe it was time to shake up his very boring and lonely life.

MARIELA HERNANDEZ DIDN'T like confrontation.

She'd had too much of it in her young life, especially during the five years of her tumultuous marriage. She'd hoped the divorce would put an end to that turmoil, but her ex-husband just refused to let go, constantly phoning her or visiting her against her wishes.

"I hope you understand we really can't have this happening here. Many of our women are still fragile because of the abuse they've suffered," her program director, Maggie, said, her voice filled with concern, but also compassion.

Maggie was a sixtysomething woman who could best be described as bohemian with her long, flowing floral tunics and earth-colored maxiskirts whose hems skimmed well-worn Birkenstocks. Her Earth Mother vibe was often a calming influence on the women staying in the halfway house and had soothed Mariela as well when she had first stayed there.

"I understand, Maggie. It won't happen again,"

she said, although she was unsure of whether or not she'd be able to keep that promise.

Maggie eyed her intently, clearly seeing past the words to what Mariela was thinking. "I know you mean that, only…" Her voice trailed off as Maggie opened her drawer, withdrew a business card and slid it across the surface of the scarred wooden desk.

"This is my good friend Elena Diaz-Gonzalez. She's an attorney who I think can help you. I know your ex-husband has money and is well-connected, but so is Elena. Go see her. Talk to her," Maggie stressed.

Mariela stared at the card but didn't reach for it immediately. She'd had enough of attorneys during her messy divorce proceedings. Even though she'd supposedly had a good one, she'd always gotten the sense that he'd been more interested in the hours on his timesheet than finalizing the divorce proceedings. But he had managed to get her a very favorable settlement that had made her new life possible.

If she could only get her ex to stop bothering her, she might actually be able to get on with her new life.

"Mariela?" Maggie pressed when she didn't take the card.

Knowing her program director wouldn't be appeased, she snatched the card off the desktop and tucked it into the back pocket of her jeans.

"I will call her. Thank you for the information," Mariela said as she stood and headed for the door. She would phone as promised, but not until she'd visited her ex and warned him one last time before she sicced another attorney on him. Especially since using an attorney would eat into the divorce settlement she'd received and which she needed to keep her parents in their assisted living facility as well as pay for her last two college semesters.

Determined to finish out her shift at the halfway house where she volunteered as a way of paying forward how they'd helped her, she returned to the day-care area where she often watched the younger children until their mothers came home from work. She loved spending time with the kids. Their joyful antics after surviving the abuse of their mothers gave her hope that she could one day be free of her nightmares as well.

The first of the moms returned and little by little the children filtered out of day care, heading to their private areas in the house as well as the common kitchen and living spaces.

She shot a quick glance at her watch. If she hurried, she might be able to catch her ex—Jorge— at his office where there would be other people around in case things went south.

Her car was in the shop for repairs, so she called a car service for the trip from the halfway house in Little Havana to the office building on Brickell Avenue where Jorge had his office. She hated doing that since being around unknown people, especially men, made her fearful, but it was too far to walk.

Barely ten minutes later, the driver dropped her off on Brickell and she hurried into the lobby of the office building where she badged herself through security. Her ex hadn't deactivated her card, clearly still in denial mode about the end of their marriage, which was why he continued to chase after her despite her many requests that he leave her alone.

There was no way she was going back to a marriage filled with both physical and emotional abuse. A marriage where she had lost herself and her dignity until she'd found the courage to stand up for herself.

Rushing off the elevator on his floor, she walked to the door of his company's business and was surprised to see that no one was at the reception desk. Even though it was just past five, Jorge often met with clients after hours and insisted on having someone in reception to greet them.

She entered the office to striking silence.

The office was totally empty, with none of the usual collection of salespeople and project developers who used to fill the space when she and Jorge had been married.

Weird, she thought and forged ahead to Jorge's corner office. There was a small anteroom where her ex's administrative assistant normally sat, but as with the rest of the office, his assistant wasn't at her desk.

The door to Jorge's office was ajar and she went to enter, but heard him speaking, his voice agitated.

She snuck a peek and realized he was on his cell phone, pacing back and forth as he spoke to whoever was on the other end of the line.

"You don't understand. This project has to go forward," he said and raked his fingers through his thick, dark hair.

A pause followed his words and then he said, "I don't care how dangerous it is. Tell me how much you want."

How much you want? As in money? Mariela thought and stepped back so Jorge couldn't see her, but she continued to listen in, worried that something bad was going on.

"Are you crazy!" Jorge almost shouted into the phone.

A pause again, shorter as he jumped in with, "I know you're taking a big risk. So am I. You've made good money with me in the past—"

Apparently cut off by the other party, Jorge shut up and sighed. Peering through the crack of the doorframe and the edge of the door, she saw him standing there, his face mottled with rage. His hand fisted at his side. The tension in his body evident.

She recognized the stance well. It was how he would look before his rage exploded and he'd start whaling on her with his fists.

"No, you listen to me. You do this and you'll get your blood money," he yelled and swiped to end the call.

She muttered a curse and stepped back, afraid that Jorge would realize that she'd heard the conversation he obviously didn't want anyone to hear. That might explain why the office was empty.

Rushing back out of his anteroom, she hurried away and walked to the front door, trying to make it seem as if she had just come in.

Jorge marched out of his office, fists clenched at his sides and his face still tinged with the angry splotches of red and white. She noticed for the first time that there were strands of white salting his dark hair and he seemed thinner. He stopped short as he noticed her by the front door and relaxed his fists, but that was only a show.

Sauntering toward her, his gaze skipped over her face, as if trying to confirm she was really there. *Or possibly how long I've been here*, she worried.

"Mariela. What are you doing here?" he said as he stopped in front of her and continued his perusal.

She gestured toward the door. "I just came in," she said and nearly bit her lip at how defensive it sounded, as if she was desperate for him to think she hadn't been there long.

"Did you now?" he said and looked away from her down toward his office, his gaze narrowed. Assessing.

Trying to distract him, she gestured to the empty office. "Where is everyone?"

He grimaced, peered around the vacant office and said, "Things have been…slow."

"I'm sorry to hear that," she said truthfully, but not because she cared for Jorge. It was more about his staff, who had generally been a nice group of people and might be suffering from the downturn in the business.

He glanced at her again, gauging her sincerity and, seemingly satisfied, he said, "What can I do for you?"

"You can leave me alone, Jorge. I'm not coming back no matter how often you call or visit," she said and braced herself for the explosion that usually came when she asserted herself.

He clenched and unclenched his hands, and the color rose on his face once more, but to her surprise, he relaxed his hands again and sucked in a deep, controlling breath. "I'm a changed man, Mari. You have to believe that," he said and held his hands out in pleading.

Maybe he was. For now, she thought as she examined his features. He'd aged in the short year and change since she'd left him. Guilt slammed into her that she was maybe responsible for that until she reminded herself that he'd regularly made her feel guilty to justify why he punished her, either verbally or physically.

Grateful for that reminder, she told herself that she didn't care if he had somehow become a better man. She wasn't willing to take the risk to find out because whatever they'd once had was long gone.

"I'm sorry, Jorge, but what we had is over. You have to accept that because—"

"I can't accept that, Mari. What we had was special," he said and reached for her, but she jumped back, unable to stand his touch.

"I have to go. Please don't come again or I'll have no choice but to contact the authorities," she said and rushed out of his office before Jorge could say or do anything else.

As she waited for the elevator, she constantly checked over her shoulder, expecting him to rush out after her, to punish her, but he didn't.

Had he believed that I had only just arrived? That I didn't overhear his conversation? she wondered. And what would happen if he didn't? The phone call had seemed urgent and not entirely aboveboard.

She'd had her suspicions more than once that Jorge had pushed projects through in shady ways, but he'd always either smooth-talked away her concern or bullied past her misgivings. Because she'd never wanted to push and unleash the monster inside him, she'd let it go, telling herself that her survival outweighed what he was doing. Especially since nothing had ever happened over the years on any of his construction projects.

But this conversation had sounded like there was major trouble and danger. Too much for her to ignore, only…

As she stepped onto the elevator, she reached into her back jeans pocket, and removed the card Maggie had given her. *Elena Diaz-Gonzalez, Attorney at Law.*

The attorney's office was right nearby in another of the buildings on Brickell Avenue. She could walk the short distance to her office, but first she had to check out the attorney. As Maggie had said earlier, her ex-husband, Jorge, was wealthy and well-connected. Mariela needed to know Ms. Diaz-Gonzalez also had influential contacts in order to deal with whatever Jorge would do.

Whipping out her smartphone, she did an internet search on the lawyer and immediately found Diaz-Gonzalez's website and bio, but that was self-serving promotion. Digging deeper, she located several articles on high-profile cases the lawyer had won. She also discovered that Elena was related to the South Beach Security family. She recognized the Gonzalez family well and hadn't realized the attorney was connected to them. The family patriarch was the equivalent of a local hero to Miami Cubans since he'd been involved in the Bay of Pigs Invasion, and the family was a prominent one in Miami. Not to mention that SBS had recently been in the news because of a human trafficking ring they'd helped stop. But unfortunately, Elena was also the wife of Jose Gonzalez, who worked in the Miami District Attorney's office.

The same DA's office that had refused to charge Jorge when he'd beaten her so badly she'd had to be hospitalized.

That made her slow her headlong flight to Elena's nearby office. But as she walked, she considered what had happened at the halfway house earlier and what she'd just overheard in Jorge's office. They were both things she couldn't handle alone, and as Maggie had said, Ms. Diaz-Gonzalez might be someone who would have the connections to help.

Sucking in a deep breath, she pulled her shoulders back and dialed the law office hoping someone was still there even though it was after five.

When a receptionist cheerily answered, she said, "I'd like to make an appointment to see Ms. Diaz-Gonzalez. Tonight, if possible."

Chapter Two

Ricky sat on the couch in his aunt's office, sharing with her what he thought about the client she had sent him for a consult. "I think she's experienced abuse based on what we discussed. Her husband regularly bullied her verbally and made her beg for money and time away from the house. He normally only let her out to do household errands and insisted on tracking her every move. There are also her accounts of how her husband would physically attack her."

His aunt Elena nodded as she sat on the couch beside him. "We have a number of police reports about visits to the home. Neighbors called in because they were worried. She was also hospitalized a number of times because of his physical abuse."

"It sounds like you have enough to build a self defense argument against the murder charge," Ricky said, considering all the evidence his aunt had gathered.

"It does and I appreciate your help. Would you

mind if I call in Dave Baker to confirm your analysis?" she asked.

He didn't mind at all. He'd only just finished getting his PhD and license while Baker was an experienced psychologist well-known for his handling of domestic abuse victims. "Baker is an excellent choice, *tia*. His opinion will carry a lot of weight with the court."

She leaned over and patted his knee. "Your opinion will be helpful also, Ricky. I see how well you're doing with the members of your support group. In no time more people will be coming to you for help and for your opinion."

"I hope so," he said, but in the meantime, he was actively building his private practice, helping his aunt and the SBS when they needed it, as well as running his support group for people suffering from trauma.

His aunt's phone rang, and she reached over and picked up the extension sitting on a table beside the sofa.

"This young lady wants to see me tonight?" *Tia* Elena said and did a quick look at her watch. With a resigned sigh, she said, "If Maggie recommended her to me, I can't refuse. Please ask her to come over as soon as she can."

"Another late night, *tia*?" Ricky asked when his aunt hung up the phone.

"Sometimes it's unavoidable," she said, stood

and held out her hand. "Thank you for helping me out."

He cupped her hand with both of his and squeezed tenderly. "Thank you for trusting me enough to give me the business. I truly appreciate it."

Tia Elena smiled indulgently. "The Gonzalez family sticks together."

"We do, but only if you think I can do the job," he said, not wanting the work if he wasn't up to it.

"Of course, Ricky. I wouldn't jeopardize my clients if I didn't think you could handle it," his aunt said and guided him toward the door to her office.

They exchanged a quick hug and a kiss on the cheek, and then he headed into the main space of the law firm where nearly a dozen attorneys and their staff worked on assorted cases.

As he neared the door, an extremely attractive young woman entered. Sun-streaked, caramel-colored hair fell in soft waves around her heart-shaped face, accenting stunning eyes of deep emerald. She was casually dressed in jeans that hugged nicely rounded hips and thighs, and a flowing tunic top that did nothing to hide her voluptuous breasts.

His gut tightened in appreciation of her natural beauty, but he reminded himself that if this was the young woman who had just called for an appointment, she was likely a survivor of domestic abuse if Maggie Alonso had given her his aunt's number.

Because of that, he gave her plenty of space as she hurried in, a wary look on her face as she saw him by the door. She was clearly leery of men, and it saddened him that she had experienced so much pain at such a young age. By his guesstimate, she couldn't be more than thirty, but then again, abuse knew no age limits.

"Mariela Hernandez," she said to the receptionist and shot a quick, suspicious look over her shoulder at him as he lingered by the entrance.

He raised his hands as if to say *We're cool* and hurried out the door, his one hope that his aunt would be able to help her.

WAY TO GO, MARI. You just chased off that poor man, her inner voice chastised, and quickly added, *And a very handsome one at that*.

Jorge is handsome, too, she reminded herself and shot another quick look over her shoulder to make sure the man had gone.

He had. She released a pent-up breath as a young woman walked up to the receptionist's desk.

"Ms. Hernandez? I'm Chelly, Ms. Diaz-Gonzalez's assistant. Would you follow me, please?" she said and gestured for her to walk down the hall. The young woman's pace was sedate and measured as they went to a large corner office at the far side of the floor.

Chelly motioned for Mariela to enter, and she did, taking a hesitant step while wringing her hands with worry.

An older woman who some might call handsome rose and held her hand out in welcome. She had dark mahogany hair with a few strands of gray, cut in a bob that accented her strong jaw. Chocolate brown eyes were filled with concern and seemed at odds with the very businesslike black suit she wore.

"Please come in, Mariela. May I call you Mariela?"

"Yes, of course," she said, walked in and perched herself on the edge of a chair, prepared to run away if things got too intense.

With an elegant wave of her hand, the woman said, "I'm Elena. I understand Maggie Alonso recommended me."

Mariela nodded. "She did. I volunteer at her halfway house."

Elena leaned back in her chair and peered at her with her sharp, brown-eyed gaze. "Maggie's a good friend. I admire what she's done to help so many with her nonprofit."

Mariela admired her as well and had been the recipient of Maggie's help in the first few weeks after she'd made the decision to divorce her husband and fled her home to escape his abuse.

"She's helped many women…women like me. When I left my husband, I didn't know what to do or where to go and Maggie took me in," Mariela said and laid a hand on her chest in emphasis.

Elena nodded and dipped her head with understanding. "Is that why you're here? Are you still having issues with your husband?"

Mariela hesitated, uncertainty about Elena's husband driving her doubts. Which was why she didn't share the main reason that had pushed her to reach out to the attorney.

"My ex…he abused me. Physically and emotionally. We divorced a little over a year ago," she said, her speech halting as emotion nearly choked her throat tight. She pushed on to finish with, "He won't stop coming around. He thinks we can reconcile and stay together."

Elena shot away from her desk and came around to sit in the cushioned chair next to Mariela. She laid a comforting hand on Mariela's thigh. "Are you concerned he'll hurt you?"

Mariela had often worried that Jorge would grow violent with Maggie or anyone who got in his way. After what had happened barely an hour earlier when she'd been in his office, Mariela also worried that he'd kill her if he thought she'd overheard his conversation.

Shakily, she nodded and said, "Yes. Either me or anyone who helps me."

With another stroke and a pat of Mariela's knee,

Elena said, "We won't let that happen." She paused for a long second and said, "Is there anything else you're worried about?"

Her mother had said that she always knew everything Mariela was thinking just from a look at her face. She wondered if Elena had that same gift and had seen that she was keeping something secret. Trying to guard against that, she looked away as she said, "No. *Nada.*"

Another protracted pause followed until Elena finally said, "We will help you, Mariela."

"We?" she croaked, confused by who else would be helping.

"Yes, we. My legal team and I will begin drafting a restraining order against your ex-husband. But we both know they're sometimes not worth the paper they're printed on, so I may call in members of SBS if I feel you're in danger."

"South Beach Security? I'm not sure I can afford them," she said, fear shooting through her at how much this all might cost. SBS usually protected the rich and famous and she was neither. Whatever money she had saved was earmarked for her dreams and taking care of her parents.

"Don't worry about the cost. South Beach Security is family and now you're family as well," Elena said, reassuring her until she continued. "There's just one thing."

Mariela clasped her hands tightly together, her palms wet with the sweat of fear. Elena reached out and covered her hands with hers. "Relax, Mariela. I think that it might be good for you to talk to someone about what you've experienced. It could help you deal with the trauma and any fears you must have. If there's anything else that's worrying you, sharing might ease your concerns."

Maggie had suggested the same thing more than once, but Mariela had always resisted, being a very private person. But as she met Elena's determined gaze, it was clear that refusing that request might not be an option. Plus, maybe it was time she shared her fears and shed the weight of them that dragged on her every day of her life. Not to mention possibly sharing what she'd just overheard about Jorge's business dealings with the proper authorities.

"I'll think about talking to someone," she said.

"Good," Elena replied, hopped out of her chair and returned to her side of the desk. She picked up her phone, dialed and a few seconds later she said, "Ricky. Are you still at the office?"

A short pause came before she said, "Yes, of course. I forgot tonight was your support group. Would you mind if someone new joined you today?"

Elena eyed Mariela with determination, and for a moment, Mariela felt like her life was spinning out of control again. But she told herself Elena was only trying to help and not just bully her.

"*Gracias.* I'll send her down in a few minutes."

When she hung up, she continued to peer at Mariela, her gaze assessing. "I suspect you feel as if I'm being pushy."

It was apparently impossible to hide anything from the sharp-eyed attorney. "I do. Jorge—my ex—used to decide things 'for my own good' as well," she said, emphasizing the words with air quotes.

Elena nodded sharply. "I appreciate you being honest with me. I leave it up to you whether or not you go to Ricky's support group, but I think sharing with others might be a good way for you to get started on your healing."

Healing. A funny word to use, but maybe the right one. She may have escaped Jorge's abuse, but inside she was often that scared woman waiting for the next blow to come. Much like she had been at the front door when the handsome man had walked by. She'd braced herself, fearful as she often was among strangers. It made the simplest things scary, like her earlier ride with the car service. She'd been apprehensive the entire time she'd been in the vehicle.

It was no way to live and maybe Elena was right that it was time to heal emotionally as well.

"*Gracias.* I will go to… Ricky, was it?" she asked.

Elena reached to a business card holder on her desk, grabbed a card and handed it to her. "Ricardo Gonzalez. He's a psychologist and his office is just a few floors down."

Another Gonzalez family member, she thought. It occurred to her then that this was possibly the SBS office building given how many Gonzalez family members had their offices here. They were a family that stuck together, something she hadn't really experienced in her life. When she'd told her parents about the abuse and her intention to ask for a divorce, they'd worried more about losing the lifestyle they'd gained as Jorge's in-laws than about Mariela's safety and happiness.

"What else do you need from me?" Mariela asked.

"We'll need your permission to obtain any police or hospital records so we can build our case to ask for the restraining order. If you don't mind coming back in the morning, we'll draft all the paperwork tonight so you can sign off."

Mariela nodded. "I assume you'll need a retainer of some kind."

Elena waved her off. "We'll have an engagement letter for you in the morning, but don't worry about the money, Mariela. You're one of Maggie's women and we'll take care of you."

"*Gracias.* I genuinely appreciate that," she said and surged to her feet.

Elena likewise stood and shook Mariela's hand. "Don't worry about anything," she repeated.

With a nod, Mariela hurried from the office

and to the elevator bank. When the elevator arrived, she hopped on for the short ride down a few floors. *Before Jorge* she would have taken the stairs to get in her steps, but *After Jorge* things like stairwells and even elevators sometimes freaked her out. Mostly because she felt like she couldn't escape them.

She counted numbers in her head as the elevator dropped, a coping mechanism that she'd found helped dampen her fear.

She'd barely reached ten when the elevator stopped.

Walking off, she searched for a sign designating the numbers on the floor and hurried toward the psychologist's office. She hesitated at the door, bracing herself for what waited for her inside, but then grabbed the knob and pushed through.

There were five people in the office, sitting around the reception area in comfy-looking sofas and chairs. It surprised her to see a man there, but then again, domestic violence wasn't limited to women.

A second later another man walked out of a door at the far end of the space.

The handsome man from earlier that night, she realized.

She muttered a curse and was about to turn around and leave when he called out, "Welcome, Mariela. We're very happy to have you here."

Chapter Three

She was going to bolt. Ricky was sure of that as the young woman took a hesitant step back, but at his welcome she stopped short and wrapped her arms around herself. He recognized the defensive gesture as well as the look of almost dread on her beautiful face.

"Please join us," he said, his tone calm, and gestured for her to take a seat, hoping she wouldn't run out.

She hesitated, but then with a stutter-step, she slowly walked to a wing chair and perched on the edge of it as if she would dash away at any moment. But then again, there were others in his group who had also started off like that. Wary. Distrustful.

To ease into that night's meeting, he sat in a chair next to another of the support group members and opposite Mariela and said, "How is everyone today?"

A murmur of responses greeted him and he eased his group into sharing how their days were going and what might be bothering them or what might be going well. Little by little the tension lessened for many of the group members, but not for Mariela, who still sat there anxiously, her body wound as tight as a violin string.

He didn't press. The release of the strain had to come naturally and only when she was ready. Too many abused women had lacked control in their lives, and it was important for her to be able to regain control again.

As the hour wore on, the others in the group shared some of what had happened to them in their daily lives and how they were coping. Or not. One of the younger women in their group, someone close in age to Mariela, explained how she had worked up the courage to leave her abusive husband. Much like he suspected Mariela had done.

With that young woman's story, he finally noticed a slight relaxation in Mariela's shoulders. He hoped that the release would continue, but Mariela's arms were still tightly wrapped around her body as if they were the only thing keeping her together. When it came time for Mariela to share, her gaze flitted around nervously and she sucked in a deep breath and held it before she blurted out, "My husband abused me, and I divorced him. He still won't let me be, but I'm not going to let him do that. I won't let him control me."

Determination filled her words, which earned commiseration and praise from the others in the group. But he sensed there were more secrets buried behind her pained gaze. More than what she had just shared.

"That's a difficult thing to do," he said, hoping she would continue the discussion and reveal whatever she was keeping private.

"It was," she said, but closed herself off again.

He didn't press even though he wanted to know more and not just on a professional level. Something about her had called his attention to her in his aunt's office. He had to admit it had been the physical at first. She was a beautiful woman. But as she'd sat there tonight, something else had intrigued him. Bothered him as well. She may have escaped her husband, but she was still hiding something. Still hurting.

Aware she wouldn't continue to share, he pressed on with the support group meeting, finishing with the last member who wasn't much more open than Mariela despite months with the group. Like Mariela, he hoped that the older woman would one day find relief from the memories that plagued her.

With their time virtually over, he ended the session. "It's almost time for when we said we'd stop, and I know you all probably want to go home because it's late. But before we go, are there any last thoughts you want to share?"

He smiled and peered around the room, but no one had anything to add. "I'm glad you all came tonight. I think we discussed some important things and I hope you'll come back next month on the 16th. Same time if that's okay with all of you."

When they all nodded, except Mariela, he stood and waited for his support group to disband. Some liked to thank him while others, still traumatized by their pasts, kept to themselves. Much like Mariela as she ducked out after a murmured, "Good night."

After the rest of the group filed out of his office, he took a moment to jot down some notes about what had been discussed by the various members.

Satisfied he had captured the key details, he closed his journal, grabbed his keys from his desk drawer and hurried out of his office and down to street level. He wanted to grab some takeout from the Cuban restaurant on the corner before he went home.

As he exited the building, he noticed Mariela standing by the curb. Since it was late and most of the business crowd in the area had gone, making the street a little empty, he walked over to make sure she was okay.

"Waiting for a ride?" he asked, and she jumped, startled, when he came up to her.

"Y-yes," she stammered, glanced at her smartphone and grimaced. "They canceled my ride."

"If you're okay with it, I can drive you home," he said and held up his keys.

"I don't want to put you out," she said and peered down at the ground, avoiding his gaze.

"It's not a problem, but if you don't want to, at least let me keep you company while you wait for another ride." She'd probably had little say about what she could do in her marital relationship, and he wouldn't do the same with her.

She nodded and fiddled with her phone again, probably placing a new request for a ride, but then she shook her head and her lips tightened in disgust. Glancing up at him, she said, "I'm having trouble getting a car. Peak hours and it's too short a ride apparently."

He held his keys up again and she took the hint. "Are you sure it's not a problem? My house is in Little Havana."

"Not a problem at all. I have to head that way to go to my place," he said and, with a sweep of his hand, pointed her in the general direction of his car. He'd pick up some food once he got closer to home.

"*Gracias*. That's very nice of you," she said. They walked together, but not really together since they were a foot apart. His Audi A4 was in the parking lot beneath his family's building.

He tapped the fob to unlock the car and walked over to open the door for her. She slipped inside and he hurried to the driver's side and got in. "What's the address?" he asked.

After she gave it, he headed down Brickell Avenue to Southwest Eighth Avenue and her home, which was located not far from some of his favorite restaurants in Little Havana. He'd pop by one on the way home to pick up dinner.

Mariela was silent during the short ten-minute drive from his family's office building to her home. He pulled up in front of the small cinderblock home just a few houses away from *Calle Ocho*. It was well-kept with a manicured front lawn, low-lying beds of colorful flowers and crotons, with taller palm trees here and there.

"Very nice," he said, but she quickly offered up a terse explanation.

"It's my parents' home. I'm trying to save my money so I can finish college and help them," she explained, obviously worried that he might think badly of her family's home.

"It's very pretty. Do you do the gardening yourself?" he asked, hoping to get her to relax and open up more about her life.

A big unrestrained smile erupted on her face. "I do. I love the colors and feeling my fingers in the dirt."

"My *abuelo* is the same way. He's 87, but he can't keep his hands out of the soil," he said, smiling as he thought about his grandfather and the remarkable gardens he had at his home.

"He sounds amazing," she said with the first hint of a smile.

"He is. Let me walk you to your door," Ricky

said and rushed out of the car. He wanted to be sure she got into her home safely. It was late and the area could be iffy at times.

"You don't have to do that," she said when he opened her door and offered her a hand to help her out of the car and onto the sidewalk.

"It's not a problem," Ricky insisted, released her hand and strolled with her to the front door. He glanced around, looking for signs of any kind of security precautions, but there were none, not even one of those simple video doorbells. Because of that, he waited as she unlocked the door and stepped inside.

The screen door closed behind her, but she turned to offer him a hesitant smile. *"Gracias,"* she said again, her face shadowed by the screen.

"Buenas noches, Mariela. I hope to see you again soon," Ricky said with a smile, hoping to build trust with her.

"Buenas noches," she said with a determined nod and closed the front door.

He started the walk back to his car, but suddenly heard something that sounded like a scream. A loud crash echoed from inside her home. The front door shook, as if hit by something. Maybe a body being slammed against it.

Ricky didn't hesitate.

He ran to the screen door and opened it. Grabbed the handle of the front door. Locked. Shouldering the door, he gave a hard shove but it held fast. He stepped back and rammed it with his shoulder, using all his strength, and it broke open, slamming against a far wall.

Glass shattered from somewhere inside the home and Mariela screamed again.

Ricky rushed deeper into her home and braced himself for an attack.

MARIELA STRUGGLED AGAINST the masked man who had assaulted her as soon as she had closed the door.

He had an arm wrapped around her waist and his gloved hand covered her mouth, muffling her screams and cutting off her air until black circles danced in her vision.

At the crash of someone breaking down the front door, the man reacted, loosening his grip slightly, and she bit down hard on his hand. The leather kept her from breaking skin, but her vicious bite made the man yelp and loosen his hold enough that she could elbow him in the stomach.

He let out a rough "Oomph" at the blow and released her. She rushed toward the front door and hopefully safety, but the man was on her again, tackling her to the ground. The weight of his body drove the air from her lungs, but a second later that weight lifted off her.

Rolling onto her side, she saw Ricky Gonzalez tossing the masked man away from her. The man stumbled back, but then regained his footing and whirled to attack again.

Ricky faced him, standing between her and her attacker. Protecting her with his body.

The man rushed at Ricky, throwing punch after punch as he tried to reach Mariela. The blows landed with sickening thuds against Ricky's face, arms and occasionally his midsection.

Ricky took the brunt of the violence, defending against the wild, almost haymaker punches of her attacker. But when their assailant paused, Ricky fought back with almost surgical precision, landing a sharp blow to the man's face that snapped the man's head back. The man reeled from the jab, but then struck out again.

Mariela screamed, "I'm calling the police."

She dialed 911 but the attack didn't stop. Ricky blocked blow after blow until the assailant gave him an opening and Ricky once again struck out, punching the other man and driving him back. That gave Ricky the space to execute a round-house kick that sent the man reeling across the room. The man stood unsteadily and raised his fists to fight again until the sound of sirens coming closer made her attacker stop short.

Before either Ricky or she could react, the man raced toward the back of the home and disappeared through the open sliding glass doors into her backyard.

Ricky came to her side, his face bloodied. His

one eye swelling shut from the masked man's blows.

"Are you okay?" he asked, apparently unconcerned about his own injuries.

"I am," she said, but suddenly her knees felt weak. She swayed, struggling to stay upright.

Ricky slipped an arm around her waist and helped her to a sofa. A second later two armed police officers rushed through the door, guns pointed and yelling, "Police." But as they saw Ricky and her sitting on the sofa, they lowered their weapons.

Ricky motioned toward the sliders and said, "He ran out the back."

One officer raced in that direction while the other holstered his gun and walked over to them. "Are you hurt?"

Mariela shook her head and glanced at Ricky, who said, "I'm fine. I need to make a call."

As Ricky walked off, the officer pulled out a pad and started asking Mariela questions about what had happened.

She answered as best she could, trying to remember everything from the moment the man had grabbed her when she'd walked in, to when Ricky had burst in to protect her.

It seemed like long minutes passed as she talked to the officer and the second policeman returned with Ricky and another man who looked so much like Ricky they had to be brothers. They had the same dark wavy hair, light eyes, straight noses and dimpled chins. But this man's body had heavier muscle, unlike Ricky's lean, almost elegant, build.

The man walked over and the police officer, who had been sitting in a nearby chair, popped to his feet. "Detective Gonzalez," he said, admiration obvious in his voice.

Ricky's brother smiled and clapped the officer on the back. "Just Trey Gonzalez now, Officer Walsh. I retired from the force last month."

Trey walked over to her, smiled and offered his hand in greeting. "I'm Ricky's older brother, Trey."

She hesitantly shook his hand. "Mariela Hernandez."

"Nice to meet you, Mariela. I'm not sure Officer Walsh has explained yet—"

"I haven't had a chance," the officer jumped in to confirm.

Trey nodded and continued. "This is a crime scene now, which means you won't be able to stay here for a few days. If you can pack up some things—"

"But where will I go?" she said, worried about not only the money if she had to stay in a hotel, but whether Jorge would come after her again. She had no doubt that Jorge had sent the man who had attacked her. And she had no doubt that if it hadn't been for Ricky, she'd be dead.

Ricky came over then, his one eye even more

swollen than before. He sat on the coffee table in front of the sofa and said, "You're coming with us. We'll make sure you're safe."

Safe. It had been so long since she'd felt safe, but as she scrutinized Trey and Ricky, she realized that if anyone could keep her physically safe, it was these two men.

But she worried that Ricky presented a different danger. In the brief time she'd known him, there was something about him that fascinated her. That threatened her on another level, but she had no choice.

Her ex wouldn't stop until she was dead, but worse than that, if he succeeded with his plan, others might die also. She had no doubt about that after the conversation she'd heard earlier that night.

She couldn't let that happen.

Chapter Four

Ricky sat in the back seat beside Mariela as Trey drove to the South Beach Security building. His body was a little sore from the attack but he hadn't felt the need for a hospital visit and an ice pack had helped ease most of the swelling around his eye. Still, a deadly silence filled the air and tension radiated from every line of Mariela's body.

She had her arms wrapped around herself tightly as if to hold herself together. Her body trembled violently, and as much as he wanted to comfort her, he suspected she wouldn't welcome his touch at the moment.

Ricky understood how she was feeling. He felt much the same way. Although his father had insisted that Trey, his sister, Mia, and he all take marital arts lessons to be able to defend themselves, he had never imagined that he'd actually have to use those skills. But he'd been able to keep Mariela's attacker at bay, even if his body and face were now suffering a little from the blows the masked man had landed.

At the building, Trey pulled into one of their reserved spots in the parking lot and hurried to help Mariela out of the car, but she shied away from his touch, obviously still traumatized. Trey understood and stepped away so she could exit the car, but he remained close by both of them, seemingly vigilant for any signs of danger.

Ricky shot him a puzzled look and Trey said, "I wanted to make sure no one followed us."

That hadn't occurred to him, making him feel a little foolish, but then again, attempted murder and mayhem weren't usually his thing. It made him wonder what he'd gotten himself into, but as he glanced at Mariela's pale and strained face, he realized he'd had no choice.

He couldn't let Mariela deal with this danger on her own.

Mindful of her mental state, he barely rested his hand at her back to guide her inside and to the elevator. At his whisper touch on her back, she jumped and glanced at him, but then relaxed a bit and offered him a tentative smile.

That smile did something weird to his insides, like ice cream melting on a scorching hot Miami day. It made him feel all soft inside.

He smiled back to reassure her as they stepped into the elevator and Trey keyed open the penthouse suite floor, which was normally only used for guests, family who worked very late and situations where they had people they had to protect since the floor was as secure as Fort Knox.

Once they were in the penthouse suite, Ricky gestured for Mariela to make herself comfortable on the sofa. As she did so, Trey stepped to one side of the room, probably to round up the rest of the team members of South Beach Security.

"How are you feeling?" Ricky asked and sat across from Mariela on the coffee table.

Mariela met his gaze but darted it nervously to Trey, who had gone over to the kitchen area in the suite.

"Mariela?" he said softly, drawing her attention back to him.

"I'm…scared. Worried," she finally admitted and ran her hands up and down her arms, as if she were cold.

Trey strolled over with a tray with three glasses of Scotch and an ice pack. He set the tray on the coffee table beside Ricky, handed him the ice pack and said, "Get that on your eye. It's swelling again and looks pretty bad."

"You should see the other guy," Ricky teased, trying to lighten the almost funereal mood. He applied the ice pack to his face, wincing at the cold and the tenderness of his cheekbone and brow.

"I wish I could. Did either of you notice anything about your attacker?" Trey asked, clearly in cop mode.

Mariela shook her head and Ricky said, "Nothing, really. About my height. Six-foot. Strong. White. I could see the area around his eyes. Hazel, I think." He circled a finger around that area on his face to show Trey how much had been visible beneath the mask.

Trey nodded, picked up a glass and handed it to Mariela. She accepted it with a shaky hand and took a tentative sip, grimacing at the strong taste of the liquor.

"Do you think your ex-husband sent this man?" Ricky asked, even though he was certain that her ex had. *But had it been to scare her into going back to him or to kill her because she'd refused him?* he wondered.

Mariela's gaze flitted from him to Trey. She took another sip, grimaced again and in a quavery voice she said, "I do."

But then she said nothing else, prompting Trey to say, "Because of your divorce?"

The ice rattled in the glass as Mariela's hands trembled violently. She avoided their gaze and in hushed tones said, "No. Because I overheard something in his office that I shouldn't have."

Ricky shared a shocked look with Trey, who continued to press. "What did you overhear?"

Her gaze locked with his and he sensed she was almost asking forgiveness, which made him reach out and lay his hand over hers. She didn't flinch or pull away, but it was impossible to miss the chill on her skin and the quiver of her muscles.

"Mariela. What did you overhear?" Ricky pressed, sure that this was what she had been keeping from him earlier.

"I'm sorry, Ricky. I never meant to bring danger to you or anyone in your family," she said, and tears leaked from her eyes and rolled down her face. She swiped at them and continued with her story. "Jorge, my ex, refused to believe our marriage was over. He kept on calling and texting me and then he came by the halfway house. It scared some of the women there."

"That's why you went to see our *tia* Elena?" Ricky said, his tone soothing and meant to encourage her to share what she had kept secret.

Mariela shook her head, surprising both him and Trey, and then she continued. "I went to see Jorge to try and talk some sense into him. But things were weird in his office. No one was there, which was unusual. When I went to Jorge's private office, I heard him talking to someone on the phone. Yelling at times because he was upset about what the other person wanted."

Trey slipped into the discussion and said, "What did that person want?"

Mariela shook her head, shrugged and took another sip of the Scotch. "If I had to guess, money. Jorge was paying them off for something. Something big."

"Something illegal?" Ricky pressed, surprised that Mariela had kept something like that from him and his aunt, but then again, maybe she hadn't felt comfortable enough to trust them with that kind of information.

MARIELA'S GUILT AT hiding her true reason had been weighing on her and she finally knew sharing it was the best thing for everyone involved. "I think so. I had worries about some of Jorge's other dealings, but he always had an excuse or made me feel like I was crazy or bullied me to stop asking. He also normally didn't involve me in his business like that."

"How did he involve you?" Trey asked, obviously wanting to get the whole picture of what the Gonzalez family had become pulled into.

Mariela shrugged and explained her role in her ex's company. "I did all the social events. I planned the parties and made sure Jorge's connections were treated right. I helped him build his network of possible investors for his various projects."

"But you had no idea of his day-to-day business dealings or projects?" Ricky asked.

She shook her head. "Not really. I mean, I knew when he was putting together another real estate deal or building a development because I had to plan the events, but nothing else. But like I said, I got the sense something wasn't right about some of them."

Trey looked at his brother and then jerked his

head toward the far side of the room. Both men rose, walked away and spoke in hushed tones, glancing at her occasionally.

It struck her once again how similar and yet different they were. Both handsome, only Trey was dark and stormy while Ricky was all brightness and light. And it was clear that darkness and light were having a major battle.

When they returned, Ricky once again sat in front of her while Trey finally took a seat at the far end of the sofa, his sea-green eyes blazing with irritation.

"Is there anything else you need to tell us?" Ricky said, his tone encouraging her to share. His gaze compassionate, in total contrast to his brother's angry look.

"Jorge said it was dangerous, and he said he'd paid this person in the past. I think it has to do with one of his new developments and I worry that people might die if we don't stop him," Mariela admitted.

"We?" Trey said with the arch of a dark brow.

Guilt slammed into her again. She'd drawn them into this trouble and understood Trey's upset.

"I didn't share this with your aunt because I didn't know if I could trust her," Mariela confessed.

"You didn't think you could trust her? But you still went to her anyway?" Trey accused, his anger clearly escalating.

"Chill, Trey," Ricky said and laid a reassuring hand on her knee. "If you didn't trust *Tia* Elena, why did you go to her?"

She glanced from Ricky to Trey and then back to Ricky. "Because I had no one else I could trust. Nowhere else I could go."

Chapter Five

Ricky's heart hurt for her, but that still didn't change the fact that his family and he were now involved and in possible danger.

"You can trust us, and you can stay here until we figure out what's going on," he said.

Mariela shot a hesitant glance at Trey, who reluctantly nodded to confirm what Ricky had said. "We will help you, but you need to share everything with us, including why you don't trust our aunt."

"Your aunt's husband—"

"*Tio* Jose?" Ricky said, confused about why she'd know him.

Mariela nodded. "Jorge beat me up pretty badly one time. Broken ribs and wrist. He punched me so hard he knocked me out. One of the neighbors heard me screaming for him to stop and called the police. When they arrived and saw my condition, they took me to the hospital and arrested Jorge, but the DA's office refused to charge him."

"The DA's office where *Tio* Jose works," Trey said, connecting the dots in her story, and continued. "There are lots of reasons why they wouldn't prosecute, mainly if you wouldn't testify."

Mariela did a little dip of her head. "I was afraid about testifying, but I got the sense that Jorge's attorneys convinced the DA that it had been the first time and that he'd go to counseling."

"Did he?" Ricky interjected.

"He went a couple of times, but I also wondered if Jorge bought his way out of it, both at the DA's and with the psychologist, since he stopped going to the sessions."

"And you think your ex also paid off people in some of his business dealings?" Ricky pressed, wanting to understand her mindset and how that was going to impact how his family could help her.

"I do. I'm worried about what I overheard. That people could be killed," Mariela said and took another sip of her Scotch.

Ricky peered at Trey and his brother's concern and anger were obvious. Despite that, his brother nodded to confirm that South Beach Security would help find out what was happening. Because of that, Ricky said, "We will help, Mariela. Let me get you settled and then Trey and I can discuss what to do next and order up some food. I don't know about you, but I'm a little hungry."

Maybe sitting around the table sharing a meal would help her relax some more and also help her grow comfortable enough to be totally honest with them.

Mariela shot to her feet, grabbed her bag and followed Ricky to one of the bedrooms in the penthouse suite.

"Feel free to put your things in here. There's a bathroom at the far end and it should be stocked with toiletries," Ricky said.

"Gracias," Mariela said and entered the bedroom while Ricky returned to his brother's side, losing some of his earlier confidence.

"You okay?" Trey asked, his gaze inquiring.

Ricky let out a rough laugh. "I think that's normally my line."

Trey chuckled and nodded. "Yeah, I think it is. So are you? Okay?"

Ricky blew out a slow breath and shook his head, which only made it hurt from where the attacker had hit him. Wincing, he said, "This isn't normally my thing, Trey. You're the hero type, not me."

With a dip of his head, his brother said, "You probably saved her life today. Seems to me that's kind of heroic."

"I had no choice," he said with unexpected anger, surprising himself and Trey.

"You have a right to be angry. You could have been killed and now our family may be in danger as well, but we have no choice but to investigate."

Ricky nodded. "You going to call everybody in?"

"I'll call *papi* and let him know what's happening. Tonight, you can use some clothes I left in the main bedroom in case I was working late. I'll round up everyone in the morning and call you so you can come down to the office to begin our investigation," Trey advised.

"Thanks, I appreciate that. I'll order in some food—"

Trey raised his hand to stop him. "None for me, thanks. Roni is off tonight and has been holding dinner for me."

"Okay. Have a good night and thanks for everything," he said and bro-hugged Trey.

Trey returned the embrace heartily, making Ricky's body ache from the blows the attacker had landed. He was sure he'd have a gallery of colorful bruises all along his midsection and face come morning.

After he pulled away, his brother pointed at his eye and said, "Put the ice back on that. You know *mami* is going to freak when she sees that shiner."

Ricky escorted his brother to the elevator bank and said, "It's not like she hasn't seen one on you more than once."

Trey laughed and shook his head. "But I'm not her Little Ricky."

He wasn't sure he was that Little Ricky anymore either. The bookworm had been tested tonight and had somehow managed to survive.

"See you in the morning," Ricky said and heard a footfall behind him as Trey entered the elevator.

Mariela had come out of the bedroom wearing loose-fitting fleece. Her arms were wrapped tight around her body again and she had a fearful look on her face.

"You're okay here. No one can come up without the key card and there's 24-hour security in the building lobby," he said to reassure her.

"I know. It's just that… This place reminds me of Jorge's Indian Creek house."

Ricky glanced around the room. It was elegantly done in a modern minimalist style that said money and luxury. He could picture the expensive furnishings in a pricey Indian Creek location. He also found it revealing that she called it Jorge's house and not her home.

"I get that it makes you feel uncomfortable. We can see about staying somewhere else in the morning," he said, thinking that his home might not be secure enough. But his family's home was on Palm Island, which was a gated community, providing the security they might need.

"*Gracias*. I'd appreciate that," she said and visibly relaxed.

"Great. Let's get some food. I was going to order from the Cuban restaurant on the corner if that's okay," he said, mindful to include her in the decision because she'd likely had little say in things during her abusive marriage.

She nodded and smiled. "I'd like that."

He pulled up a menu on his phone and they decided on what to eat. He placed the order and got some sodas out of the fridge they kept stocked for whoever was staying in the suite. While they waited for the food delivery, they chatted.

"You mentioned you were going back to school. What's your major?" Ricky asked.

Mariela hesitated as she set a fork on a napkin. "I had been premed, but I dropped out after I married Jorge. Now that I'm enrolled again, I decided to go into marketing. I did so much of it anyway for Jorge's business and I have the connections that might help me get a good-paying job."

Money being important apparently despite her divorce settlement. It made him recall her earlier comments about her parents. "You help your mom and dad, right?"

Her hand shook again as she finished setting the cutlery on the table. "I do. They're in an assisted living facility. Their health has declined in the last few years."

Something about the way she said it made him say, "That's a big responsibility."

A careless shrug was her answer. He didn't get to question her about it more since the lobby called to announce that their order had arrived.

"I'll be right back," he said and walked to the elevator to head to the lobby to get the delivery.

MARIELA HAD NO doubt that Ricky had picked up on her ambivalence about her parents. His training as a psychologist would assist him in seeing what she wasn't saying. But what she was feeling about her parents and how they'd made her feel in return was something she didn't want to discuss because it was too hurtful. After all, how was she supposed to feel about parents who'd been willing to keep her in an abusive relationship so they'd be taken care of?

She drove those thoughts out of her mind, hoping to keep them away from Ricky's keen eyes.

When he returned a few minutes later, she forced a smile to her face as he walked to the table with their order.

"It smells delicious," she said, hoping to keep the discussion from anything too personal.

Ricky lifted an eyebrow in question, clearly aware of what she was doing, but played along with it.

"It's a great restaurant. I often pick up a meal there on my way home," he said and laid the take-out containers on the table.

"I guess you don't like to cook?" she said and removed the cover from an order of rice.

Ricky shook his head. "I love to cook, but it

seems silly to do it just for me. Especially when I work late."

She didn't need to be a psychologist to draw conclusions from what he'd said, and before she could stop herself, she said, "No girlfriend?"

He met her gaze directly and she noticed for the first time the shards of green and darker blue in his intense light blue eyes. She noticed the pain there as well.

"Not anymore. She couldn't handle my hours. Truthfully, I think we only stayed together so long because of my family," he admitted.

His Gonzalez family was well-known to most Miamians and quite successful. She'd even met his cousin Pepe on various occasions because he was an up-and-coming real estate agent who had often attended their functions.

"I imagine it can be hard for people to see you for you and not your family," she said as she uncovered the last dish for their meal.

A grunt was his only reply as he took a seat at the table and scooped roast pork, rice and beans onto his plate and then added some ripe plantains. He immediately dug into his meal, and she did the same, hunger rousing with the enticing smells wafting off the food. The citrus, cumin and garlic from the pork, earthiness of the beans and the enticing sweetness of the ripe plantains.

She devoured the food on her plate in no time, surprising herself because she hadn't expected to be hungry with all that had happened that night. When she finished, she reached for seconds at the same time he did. Their hands collided over the black beans and, at the touch, an unexpected feeling zapped through her: comfort.

They both pulled away slowly, and as she met his gaze, Ricky said, "It will be okay, Mariela."

"Will it?" she said, doubtful that even the powerful Gonzalez family could accomplish that. The anger that had been simmering in her over the years of her marriage and after her divorce finally erupted. "I told myself it would be okay when Jorge started with his nasty comments. But it only got worse. I told myself my parents would support me, only they didn't. And now… I can't even think about how this is all not okay," she said, her throat choking up with the release of the emotions she had kept bottled up for so long.

Ricky cupped her cheek, and to her surprise, she didn't jerk back as she so often did after the years of abuse. As it had before, that sense of comfort filled her and tamed the heat of the emotions that had swept over her.

Beneath his palm Ricky felt the tempering of the rage that had overtaken her just moments before. He stroked her cheek with his thumb to reassure her about his words.

"I can't imagine how hard it's been for you.

But we are here for you, and we will make sure you're safe," he said and genuinely believed that his family could do just what he had promised.

"I know you believe that," she said, her voice breaking with worry.

"I do. I may not be like Trey—"

"You may not think you are, but I see it differently," she said, covered his hand with hers and drew it away from her face to twine her fingers with his. "I don't think I'd be alive right now if it wasn't for you."

He didn't think so either and, unfortunately, he was also sure that they weren't done with being in danger. Whoever had sent the masked man tonight was likely to keep on trying to silence Mariela. His one hope was that he'd be up for the challenge of keeping her safe.

With a gentle squeeze of her hand, he said, "It's late. You should go get some rest."

She nodded but said, "I'll help you clean up."

"No need. I can handle it myself," he said, imagining that in Mariela's life she'd had few people who'd taken care of her. Plus, he needed time alone to think about all that had happened and prepare himself for tomorrow.

A ghost of a smile finally drifted across her face. "*Gracias*. I appreciate that. I'm not used to…" Her voice choked up and she forced herself to finish. "It's been a long time since someone was nice to me."

He wanted to say that it was a shame that she'd lacked that in her life but bit it back. He didn't want her to think he was pitying her or making a play. She was too vulnerable for that.

"We'll meet with my family in the morning, and you'll need to be sharp so we can figure out what we need to do about your ex."

With a small nod, she slipped her hand from his. Despite his earlier words, she grabbed her dirty plates and cutlery and walked them over to the sink before heading to her bedroom.

He likewise picked up his dirty dishes and brought them over to the kitchen. He threw out the take-out containers and loaded the dishwasher.

The simple, homey tasks made him stop short and lean on the counter heavily. There was nothing simple or homey about the situation he'd been pulled into. He needed to regroup and prepare himself for tomorrow and whatever else was coming their way. And he needed to get more ice on his face because his mother was going to freak for sure when she saw him in the morning.

He made himself a fresh ice pack and headed to what would be his bedroom for the night.

As he lay in bed in his brother's too-large sweats, he worried the challenge ahead would likewise be too large for him to handle. But he told himself he could handle it. That the same vein of strength that ran through his grandfather, father and Trey ran through him as well.

He was just a different kind of hero, not that he'd ever thought of himself in that role. But he intended to be ready for the challenge, he told himself over and over again as he lay in bed, hoping to convince himself of the truth of those words by morning.

JORGE HERNANDEZ PACED back and forth across his living room, worry and anger twined together in his gut like a viny weed as he waited for word from his man.

He'd tried calling the burner phone he'd given his old foreman a few times, but the man hadn't answered. Jorge didn't know whether that meant something had gone wrong, or if he was being as unreliable as he had been when he'd worked for him.

He should have gotten someone else to do the job, only he hadn't had time to find anyone else.

Cursing, he dialed again, hand fisted around the phone tightly as it rang and rang.

No one answered.

The pressure built in his head and the fire of rage kindled in his gut until it exploded like a volcano spewing lava.

He tossed the phone against the wall where it shattered and fell onto the cold marble floor in pieces that reminded him of the state of his life.

He'd once had everything. A successful business. A beautiful wife and home.

But now all that was left of his life were the broken pieces, never to be put back together again. He knew that now. There was no going back to his old life, and he had to make sure Mariela wouldn't talk and ruin his plans for the future.

Chapter Six

It is more than a little intimidating to be sur-rounded by some of Miami's most prominent and wealthy individuals, Mariela thought as she sat at the conference room table the following morning.

Tia Elena sat beside Ricky's father, Ramon, the current head of South Beach Security, and Ricky's mother, Samantha. It had been impossible to miss the worry on Samantha's classic features when she'd first seen Ricky's bruised face. Truth be told, Mariela had also been shocked by the kaleidoscope of purple and blue along his cheek and the deeper black beneath Ricky's eye.

An attractive woman with sun-streaked light brown hair sat beside Trey in a dark black suit that screamed cop. His fiancée, Roni, she guessed. She vaguely recalled seeing a photo of her in the news article about the human trafficking ring Trey and she had broken up just a couple of weeks ago.

Mia Gonzalez was next at the table together with her cousin Carolina Gonzalez. The Twins, as they were known to the family and many others in Miami, were social media influencers invited to all the top events and, as always, they were dressed to the nines in designer sundresses. She'd had them to Jorge's parties on a few occasions and they'd always been pleasant. She wondered how they could possibly help in this situation, but then again, SBS had its own way of getting things done.

The last two people at the table, a man and woman with the unmistakable Gonzalez looks, were twenty somethings with open laptops sitting before them. They were dressed casually, the man in a button-down Oxford shirt while the woman wore a simple, pale peach blouse.

Unlike last night when he'd been in a *guayabera* shirt and jeans, Trey wore a dark blue pinstriped suit with an electric white shirt and red tie. He rose from the table and formally introduced everyone seated at the table.

"I think you already know *Tia* Elena. My father, Ramon, is the head of the agency, and my mother, Samantha, is our Mama Bear," he said with sincere affection and continued.

"My fiancée, Roni. She's a detective with Miami Beach PD," he explained, his voice filled with pride and love.

He gestured to the Twins. "I think you've probably met Mia and Carolina. They know everyone who's anyone in Miami, which comes in handy a lot."

With another wave of his hand at the direction of the two twentysomethings, he said, "Sophie and Robert Whitaker, our cousins. They're top tech gurus and ethical hackers. If they can't find it or break into it, no one can."

Ricky laid his hand on hers as it rested on the tabletop. "This is the heart and soul of South Beach Security, Mariela. We will protect you," he said.

"Thank you, everyone. I appreciate all that you've done so far, but I'm not sure I can afford—"

Ramon held his hand up to stop her. "That's not how we work, Mariela. Besides, Ricky is involved in this now also and we always protect our family."

She shot a quick glance at Ricky, who nodded in confirmation. "I don't know how to thank you. This is all so…crazy. I mean, Jorge has been violent in the past, but this…it's a whole new level of crazy."

"People get that way when money is involved. Especially big money," Trey said.

"Do you have any idea what projects your ex-husband is currently developing?" Ramon asked.

Mariela shook her head. "I haven't been involved at all since our divorce."

"It makes sense to call in Pepe," Ricky said, but that prompted uneasy murmurs around the table since all of them knew Pepe didn't like to be involved in agency business.

"I'll call Pepe. He won't say no to me," Ramon said, ending the discussion.

"I'm sure Robbie and I can also get that information," Sophie said and shot a quick look at her brother, who confirmed it with a nod.

"All right," Ricky said and sat back as Trey assumed control of the meeting.

"Roni. Can you get us a copy of any evidence that Miami PD has about the attack last night?" Trey asked.

"It depends on which detectives are handling it, but hopefully I can," his fiancée replied.

"Good. Back to the new construction developments. My guess is that whoever your ex is paying off works as an inspector of some kind. Did you ever meet any of the inspectors on the various projects?" Trey asked.

With a shrug, she said, "Some of them occasionally attended Jorge's holiday parties. I may still have the invite lists on my laptop or in my old planner. The planner is still in my parents' house."

"Will Miami PD let us back into the house?" Ricky asked, concerned about being able to access the planner.

"We can call PD to request access to the crime scene," Roni said and then muttered a curse and apologized. "I'm sorry, Mariela. I didn't mean to be insensitive."

"It's okay, Roni. I'm not sure I'll be able to think of it as my home for a long time," Mariela admitted. A chill filled her as she remembered being assaulted the second she walked into her family home.

IT WAS IMPOSSIBLE for Ricky to miss Mariela's upset. Her hand had tightened against his as he held it, mirroring the growing tension of her body.

He gave her hand a reassuring squeeze. "We will help you get through this."

She offered up a weak smile. "I can probably make a partial list if we can't get the planner or it's not on my laptop. Possibly the names of some of the special inspectors and structural engineers as well."

"We can check to see if any of the reports are available to the public," Robbie said and began tapping away on the laptop. With a small hoot and a laugh, he said, "Look at that. The inspection reports are all online. I just need the addresses."

"You were worried there was something shady going on with some of the projects. Do you remember which ones?" Ricky asked Mariela.

Mariela tightened her lips and did a little bobble with her head. "Maybe. I can think of at least two where I thought something was off."

"Great. Let's start with those. If you can give the addresses to Sophie and Robbie, we'll dig through the reports later and start making a list of suspects," Trey advised and clapped his hands as if to say *Let's get going.*

Sophie and Robbie closed their laptops and shot to their feet, eager to get to work.

Roni rose and walked over to Trey, who laid a possessive hand at her waist. She dropped a quick kiss on his lips. "See you later," she said.

"Stay safe," Trey said and swept his hand across her back lovingly.

"You, too," Roni said before she hurried out the door.

The obvious love between the two caused an ache in the middle of her chest. When she had first married Jorge, they'd had that kind of love. Or at least she thought they'd had. The illusion had disappeared like the wisps of smoke from a candle that had just been blown out.

Trey peered at Ricky. "If you two could make those lists, it'll give us more to work with," he said.

"Will do," Ricky agreed.

"I'll be in my office, getting settled," Trey advised and pointed a thumb to the door of the conference room.

As he walked there, his father met him and clapped him on the back. "You did well, Trey."

Trey smiled. *"Gracias, papi."*

After Trey had left, Ricky's dad looked at them and said, "Do you need anything else right now?"

Ricky peeked at her from the corner of his eye,

did a little cough of discomfort and said, "I was hoping Mariela and I could stay with you. The penthouse is a little…intimidating."

"Of course, Ricardo. When do you want to come over?"

"I have to get my car. We left it at Mariela's since Trey drove us here last night," Ricky said.

His mother fluttered her hands to wave him off. "We'll arrange for someone to get the car. Do you need anything else?"

Ricky once again looked at Mariela and she shook her head. "I was able to pack some things last night and I guess we'll have to wait for the police to let us back in to get the planner."

"Trey lent me some clothes he had in the penthouse, but I'd like to get some clothing from my home," Ricky told his mom.

Samantha nodded. "We can run by your house on the way to our house so you can pick up whatever you need."

"Great," he said, and everyone left the table to get to work.

When they neared the door, Ricky's mother lightly cupped his bruised cheek and said, "This looks like it hurts."

"Only when I smile," he said and grinned, but then immediately winced, seemingly forgetful of his injury.

"Oh, Ricky. I never thought I'd see you look

like this," his mom said with worry and a final stroke of his cheek.

Embarrassed color rushed across his face, and he shot a look at Mariela, obviously wishing he could crawl into a hole to avoid the babying.

She understood, but how she wished her parents would show her that kind of love now, the way they used to before worries about health had changed everything.

When Ricky's mother and father finally left the room, Mariela leaned close and whispered, "You're lucky to have that much love."

He chuckled, did a little half grin that had him wincing again and said, "I am."

With that, they headed off to his parents' car and did a quick side trip to a beautiful waterfront home in nearby Gables by the Sea. His father pulled his Jaguar sedan into the circular driveway of the sprawling ice white ranch house.

Low bushes lined the periphery of his home, their deep emerald color a contrast to the bright pink and white flowers in the planting beds and the brighter green of the lawn. Two large aqua-colored planters added yet more color as they stood sentry at either side of the patio by the front door.

Ricky was about to jump out of the car, but his father laid a hand on his arm to stop him.

"We'll go in with you," Ramon said, clearly worried that whoever had attacked her the night before might also know who had saved her and be waiting in Ricky's home.

But Ricky held his hand up and said, "I can handle this. There's no need to worry."

HE APPRECIATED HIS parents' concerns, but for far too long it had also made him feel as if he didn't quite measure up to the Gonzalez men standards.

Last night had given him his first inkling that his feelings might have been wrong. Not that he intended to be dead wrong by placing anyone in danger. He had a security system in place, and it hadn't been tripped. It was also highly unlikely that whoever had attacked Mariela last night had hung around to get his name. Still, if Mariela's husband had a connection in the DA's office or even the police, he might have been able to get that info.

Because of that, he entered his home with caution. The alarm was engaged, and nothing seemed out of place in the areas visible from the door. Disarming the security system, he waved to his father that all was clear, and his parents and Mariela walked into his home to wait for him to pack.

He hurried up the stairs to his bedroom and quickly filled a bag with what he'd need for at least a week. Not that he thought it would take that long for SBS to get to the bottom of what was happening with Mariela's ex-husband.

As a member of the agency's team, he intended

to help in whatever way he could so that Mariela could get on with her life.

On a professional level, he wanted to help her heal from the abuse she had suffered at the hands of her ex. But as a professional, he wasn't supposed to become involved with a client. That was at odds with the instant attraction that he'd felt for her. Only was she really a client based on just one visit to his support group?

That conflict is one I'm going to have to work out for myself, he thought as he finished packing.

He rushed down to where his parents and Mariela sat in the living room, seemingly making small talk. But if he knew his parents, they were conducting their own kind of interrogation.

That was confirmed as he heard his mother say, "How long were you married?"

"Five years."

"How did you meet him?" his mother asked.

"I met Jorge when I was working part-time as a hostess at a local restaurant. Jorge was a regular customer. He was handsome and always charming. He treated me well at first."

Ricky had heard similar stories way too often from his patients and some of the people in his support group. Things usually started well, but then disintegrated as either stress or just time revealed the real nature of the abuser.

"Mami," Ricky said in a tone that warned his mother to cease her inquisition.

"Just getting to know Mariela, *mi'jo*," she said with an arch of a perfectly plucked brow.

"Give her a chance to breathe, *mami*," he warned, and with a slight dip of her head, his mother acquiesced, and Mariela released a relieved sigh.

They were about to step outside when Ricky caught sight of motion from the corner of his eye. A black BMW had pulled up in front of his home. A masked driver got out of the car, and some kind of internal warning system made him sweep his arm across his father, mother and Mariela as they were about to open the door.

"Get down," he shouted.

His father opened his arms wide and pulled the women to the ground. Ricky threw his body over all of them, trying to shield them from danger.

A second later a spray of gunfire shattered the glass in the front windows and plowed into the metal front door.

It seemed like forever that the shooting went on, destroying everything in the path of the bullets. Glass shattered on nearby picture frames. Ceramic lamps exploded from the gunshots. The duller thud of bullets smashing into the door, walls and books made his body jump as he imagined them slamming into their bodies.

Luckily, they were safely on the floor and behind the protective metal of the front door.

As quickly as it had begun, the gunfire stopped,

and a squeal of tires signaled that the shooter had driven off. Barely a few minutes later, the wail of police sirens said that the cavalry had arrived.

Ricky stood and helped his father, mother and Mariela to their feet. As he made sure the women were okay, his father partially opened the door. Seeing the officer rushing toward the house, his father threw it open to let him in.

"Are you okay, *mami*?" he asked as his mother smoothed her blouse into place and ran a shaky hand through her hair.

"I am. Mariela?" his mother asked and glanced at the young woman.

"I'm good," she said and slowly spun to look all around.

"Your beautiful home. I'm so sorry, Ricky," Mariela murmured and covered her mouth with her hands. Tears shimmered in her gaze as she skipped it over the broken pieces of his belongings.

"It's just things," he said, even though it hurt to see the damage to the objects he had gathered so carefully to make the house his home.

"Is everyone okay?" the first officer asked and holstered his gun when he realized there was no threat from them. The officer's eyes widened as he realized who was inside. "Mr. Gonzalez. I didn't realize this was your home."

"It's my son's," Ramon said and gestured to Ricky.

"We're all fine," Ricky said and wished he could say the same about his living room and office, which had taken the brunt of the attack. The gunfire had broken a number of items in addition to the windows, and bullet holes peppered the walls, sofas and built-ins.

But what bothered him most was the very real possibility that either a cop or someone in the DA's office had revealed his name and address to Mariela's attacker. How else would someone have known where they might go?

As his gaze locked with his father's, it was clear he was thinking the same thing.

Chapter Seven

His father whipped out his cell phone and dialed. When someone answered, he said, "We have a leak, Trey. Someone just shot up Ricky's home."

The murmured sound of a few choice curses was audible before his father said, "We're all okay, *mi' jo*. As soon as we finish with the officers, we're heading home."

There was another curt response from Trey and his father nodded. "A security detail would be welcome. Can you call your contacts at PD and see what they have to say?"

A second later his father ended the call and faced the officer. "I know you have a job to do. How can we help?"

The officer nodded and took out his notepad. "Can you tell me what happened?"

Ricky motioned to the front window of his office. "I caught sight of a car pulling up and something about it worried me."

"Can you tell me what kind of car?" the officer asked.

"Late-model BMW. Black. Masked driver got out and I could see he had a rifle before we all hit the ground," Ricky said.

After jotting down the notes about the car and driver, the officer continued peppering them with questions, getting statements from each of them. When he was done, he called for a CSI unit to come and collect evidence and secured the scene with yellow police tape.

When they stepped outside, there was another police car with officers holding back a small crowd of neighbors who had come to see what had happened as well as two sets of security guards and Trey.

He rushed over as they cleared the police tape and examined them carefully, as if to reassure himself that they were all truly unharmed. Satisfied, he said, "I've got two guards to follow you back to the house. Since it's gated, you should be fine once you clear security there. The other two guards will sit here until the CSI folks are finished and then put up plywood until we can get some repairs done."

"Thanks, Trey," Ricky said and hugged him, but his brother held him just a little longer and squeezed just a little harder.

"You've got to stop scaring the life out of me," he whispered into his ear.

"Believe me, I wish I could," Ricky said and stepped back to stand beside Mariela, who had clearly retreated into herself with the violence of the attack. She'd gone back to wrapping her arms around herself tightly and worried her lower lip with her teeth. All traces of color were gone from her face, which was almost a sickly green color.

He swept his hand across her back. "It's going to be okay."

Mariela only nodded, as if she didn't trust herself to speak.

"We're going to be safe at my parents'. I promise," he said, and all she did was nod again, the action stiff.

"Let's get you there and then we can meet with Sophie and Robbie. They've gotten some info from Pepe and the building department website," Trey said.

Ricky nodded and applied gentle pressure on Mariela's back to direct her to his parents' car. Silence reigned during the short drive onto the highway, the McArthur Causeway, and finally the security gate for Palm Island. Trey was in the lead in his restored vintage Camaro while a Suburban with their security detail guarded their rear.

Once on the island they'd be safe from any land attack, but not from the air or water. An air attack seemed unlikely, but anyone could drive a boat through the canal that opened into Biscayne Bay behind the home.

As he got out of the car, he met Trey and gestured to the back of the house. "What about the dock?"

Trey nodded. "It's not likely, but there's no sense taking any chances. We'll have the guards take positions there. Good call."

"Learned from an expert," he said with a smile, fighting back a wince from his sore cheek.

THE OBVIOUS AFFECTION and respect between the two brothers helped ease some of Mariela's upset from the earlier attack. That and passing through the secured gate as well as the armed guards and the Gonzalez family. Since Trey was a retired police officer, she trusted that he was capable of arranging for the protection they needed. Ricky's father also, but what impressed her more was how Ricky was rising to the challenge.

He had been the first one to notice something was off and keep them from walking out into a hail of gunfire.

Ricky had saved her life. Again. His parents also, but they didn't seem fazed by all that had happened. Not even his mother. Maybe because as the Mama Bear of South Beach Security she was used to things like this.

As Mariela's gaze met Samantha's, his mother smiled gently and held her hand out to Mariela. "Let's get you settled while the men work out the details."

Mariela nodded, but at the door, she paused to

look back at the men as they stood in the court-yard in front of the home. It was then she realized that a beautiful wrought-iron gate protected the mouth of the driveway, and a matching fence surrounded the property, providing security for the home. The floral motif in the gate and fence were mirrored in the wrought iron of the double doors at the entrance to the house.

The home was a bright white color against the myriad greens of the palms, grass and other plants in the surrounding landscape. Brightly hued flowers were interspersed here and there, helping to break up the austerity of the white of the house and black of all the wrought iron.

Samantha led her into a large foyer and hall done in brilliant white again. For a second it reminded her of Jorge's home once more, but as she walked in, the white and black of the wrought iron on the stairways and landing was warmed by the rich wood of what had to be antique Colonial Spanish furniture and a beautiful family portrait above a massive stone fireplace.

"Your home is lovely," she said, doing a slow twirl to take it all in.

"We're lucky to have it and lots of family to fill it," Samantha said and then quickly tacked on, "And friends like you."

She wasn't sure she could think of herself as Ricky's friend, but she hoped that might happen in the future once they got to know each other better. She ignored the little voice in her head that said Ricky was the kind of man who could become more. If she could ever get over what Jorge had done to her.

Samantha guided her up the stairs to a large central landing laid out with a comfortable seating area that overlooked the living room downstairs and had amazing views out windows facing the back of the house. A canal, the Port of Miami and Biscayne Bay were visible beyond just a short distance away. A large cruise ship sat in the port, waiting for people to board.

With a wave of her hand, Ricky's mother said, "Ricky and you will be over in this guest wing. Ramon and I are on the other side of the floor if you need anything."

"*Gracias.* I really appreciate you being kind enough to do this for me," Mariela said and followed Samantha into the one room. It was an immense space with large windows on one wall and French doors onto a small balcony that faced the backyard with its water views. She noticed the two guards policing the grounds at the edge of the property and a speedboat at a dock on the canal. From this side of the home a beautiful pool and patio were also visible on the grounds below.

"Anything for Ricky and his friends," Samantha said, but Mariela didn't fail to detect the notes of worry woven into her voice.

"I never meant to bring this danger to your

home or your family," she said, tightening her hands on the handle of her overnight bag.

Samantha laid a hand on hers. "Sadly, we've faced danger before. It comes with running something like SBS."

Mariela relaxed beneath his mother's gentle touch, but it only assuaged her guilt a little bit. Not to mention that she couldn't imagine living with that kind of danger every day.

Samantha must have seen what she was thinking since she said, "Having family at your side makes it easier. I get the sense you haven't had that in some time."

Mariela couldn't disagree. "My parents haven't been well and that's changed a lot in our relationship."

"You have us now. We will get to the bottom of this," she said and quickly added, "I'll leave you to get comfortable."

"Gracias," she said again, grateful for everything that this group of virtual strangers was doing for her. It made her feel like she had a family again, something that had been lacking in recent years due to her parents' illness and Jorge's abuse.

She quickly put away the few things she had packed, stepped out of the room and literally ran into Ricky, who was leaving the room across the way from her. He grabbed her as they collided to keep her from falling.

Her instincts took over and she instantly recoiled even though his touch was surprisingly gentle.

He released her immediately, obviously aware of her discomfort. "Are you okay?" he asked.

"I am. It's just that... I'm not used to a man being...caring," she admitted and a sudden wave of sadness washed over her.

He reached for her again, intending to comfort her, but then pulled back, clearly mindful of her issues. With a flip of his hand, he motioned toward the stairs and landing. "They're waiting for us downstairs. Sophie and Robbie have some info for us. Roni also."

She hurried down the stairs, but on the ground floor deferred to Ricky, who guided her to a study in a large wing at the front of the home. There was a small conference table off to one side of the room and an ornately carved wooden desk on the other. Two of the walls were lined with bookshelves packed with books and memorabilia while the third wall boasted an immense television, sound system and computer equipment. The final wall had numerous windows that faced the front courtyard of the property and the lush gardens along the edges of the property.

Trey and his father, Ramon, were already seated at the table and a young housekeeper was setting out a coffee service on a bar cart in one corner of the room.

Both men rose as she entered. Apparently, manners had not disappeared in the Gonzalez family.

Ramon said, "Please help yourself to some coffee or tea. If you'd like anything else, please let Josie know."

Josie grabbed a coffee cup and carafe, but Mariela waved her off. She was too edgy as it was, and the coffee would only make her even more jittery.

Ricky took a cup and Josie poured him some coffee. When he smiled and thanked her, the young woman blushed and grew awkward. Josie clearly had a crush on the youngest Gonzalez family member. Mariela understood. Ricky was handsome, intelligent, caring and brave.

Seemingly too good to be true and that scared her a little because Jorge had seemed that way at first also.

When Ramon sat down at the table, Mariela did as well. Once Trey and Ricky had joined them, their father quickly dipped his head in silent command. Trey video-called his cousins, who immediately answered, their faces filling the large television on the wall.

"Good to see you all in one piece," Robbie said, earning an elbow from Sophie.

"Ignore him. He spends too much time with the computers," Sophie said in apology.

Robbie did an eye roll. "Says the woman who named her PC Blanche after her favorite Golden Girl."

Sophie released an exasperated sigh and said, "We have some information that Pepe got from the Multiple Listing Service entries."

"Does that include new construction?" Trey asked.

Sophie nodded. "It does include new construction if the builder lists it. So there may be a new development that's not yet in the MLS," she explained.

"Do you know if your ex regularly listed new projects?" Ricky asked.

"He almost always did. It was a way to keep the cash flow stable," Mariela said, but then blurted out, "But Jorge told me last night that things have been slow."

Trey tapped his pen against a pad of paper. "How slow?"

With a shrug, Mariela said, "The office was empty last night. I'd never seen it like that. There always used to be someone in there working. But it could have been he didn't want anyone to overhear his conversation."

"Like you did," Ramon said.

"Like I did. I tried to make it seem like I'd just walked in, but I guess Jorge didn't buy it," she admitted.

"It must be pretty important to him to have you killed," Ricky said, his brow furrowed in concern.

Mariela ran some of the development numbers for past deals she remembered through her head.

"A mid-rise building with about 200 units could make Jorge about 5 million. If it was a big high-rise project, he could make 10 million or more," she advised.

"Enough to kill for," Robbie chimed in with a low whistle.

Beside him Sophie flipped through a pile of papers; her lips pursed with frustration. "We have only one high-rise project on the MLS listing Pepe provided," she said.

Trey tapped his pad of paper again. "Can you send that list over for Mariela to review?"

"Sure thing," Robbie said and then continued. "If Mariela can identify any of the projects she thinks had issues, we can get the names of the inspectors so you can investigate them."

"*Gracias.* We will get to work on it as soon as we receive it. You had news for us as well, Trey," Ramon said and peered at his oldest son.

"Roni talked to the officers who had investigated when her ex put Mariela into the hospital. They seemed angry that the DA wouldn't press charges but said there was nothing they could do about it. They gave Roni a copy of the file and the name of the DA. The detectives had some choice words about how often they had issues with this DA letting people go."

"Even with violent crimes?" Ricky asked, clearly frustrated about what had happened to her.

"Even in cases where the perp was armed and

dangerous, and then they wonder why the crime rate goes up," Trey said, even more frustrated than his younger brother.

"This DA who won't charge people is the one who let Jorge go?" she asked, wanting to be sure she was understanding what had happened.

Trey blew out an exasperated sigh and said, "Apparently it is. I guess we can ask *Tio* Jose about him. Maybe Sophie and Robbie can dig into his record as well."

Tio *Jose*, Tia *Elena's husband*, Mariela thought. He had been the reason she had hesitated to approach Elena at first. It relieved her worries that Elena's husband hadn't been the one to drop the charges, but it still angered her that the DA's office hadn't pursued the case.

Ricky tentatively laid a hand on her shoulder and gave a reassuring squeeze. "We will get to the bottom of why he wasn't charged."

She wanted to say it was water under the bridge, but it did matter. "I want to know why, so someone else doesn't suffer the way I did."

HER WORDS WERE a testament to the kind of person she was. Someone willing to sacrifice herself to help aging parents. Someone who cared more for others than herself. Someone brave enough not to shrink even in the face of the abuse as well as the attacks on her life.

"We will make sure of that," he said and meant

it. Whatever it took, he would push to make sure violence against women wouldn't be ignored by that DA again.

Mariela's face reflected her concern, but with his words, a wave of release seemed to wash over her. But it was also clear she wanted to move on from that memory as she said, "I'll get to work on the MLS list as soon as we get it."

A bing on the laptop in front of Trey drew everyone's attention. After a few taps, Trey smiled and said, "I think you got your wish, Mariela."

Chapter Eight

"Great. Mariela and I will get to work," Ricky said, but then bit it back, remembering that Mariela might have control issues. Deferring to her, he said, "If that's okay with you."

She nodded. "It is."

Ramon peered around the table and said, "Trey and I will leave you to work on the list. We'll be at the office if you need us."

"We will work on it immediately," Mariela said, her determination obvious.

"Great. Like *papi* said, we'll be at the office," Trey said, a bit of annoyance in his tone, and it made Ricky wonder if his brother was finding it difficult to play second fiddle to their father. As a lead detective, Trey was used to calling his own shots, but then again, he'd had to answer to his chief on cases as well.

After the two men had left, Ricky walked to the printer to get the list and returned to the table with it. He placed it in front of Mariela and sat down beside her.

"You ready?"

MARIELA WASN'T SURE she was ready, but she had to help this investigation in any way she could, especially since she was responsible for drawing the Gonzalez family into this dangerous situation.

She grabbed a highlighter from an organizer in the center of the table and started her review of the MLS listings. The new construction projects were unfamiliar to her, but she drew a star next to a high-rise project.

"This one is 400 units right across from the beach. Luxury condos as well. If Jorge could get that to sell out it could easily make him 15 million or more," she said.

"It's a great neighborhood and oceanside. I can't imagine it wouldn't sell out," Ricky said as he leaned close to look at the entry.

Mariela screwed her eyes nearly closed as she tried to recall things she'd overheard on other projects when she'd helped Jorge with the events and marketing. "To build something like this he'd need lots of cash. Forty to 50 million is my guess."

"And you don't think he has that?" Ricky said and took another look at the MLS listing.

"When we divorced a year ago, Jorge was already pleading poverty. I thought it was just a ploy to reduce the settlement he'd have to pay me, but maybe it wasn't," she said with a shrug.

"What about presales of the units? Wouldn't they help?" Ricky wondered.

"With enough of them presold it would be easier to get the funding he needs from a bank," she said.

"I know who might be able to give us that info," Ricky said and whipped out his cell phone.

Mariela guessed that it was his cousin and that was confirmed as Pepe's voice came across the speaker.

"What can I do for you, *primo*?" Pepe said, but then quickly added, "As long as it doesn't get me shot at."

"I guess you heard about this morning," Ricky said with a grimace.

"I think most of Miami has heard. It was on the local news at lunchtime, and I suspect it'll be on the evening news as well," Pepe said.

"Great," Ricky muttered, but then pressed on. "I've got Mariela Hernandez with me. We were wondering if you knew how many units had sold on her ex's new condo development near Bal Harbour."

"Let me check," his cousin said, and Mariela heard the tap-tap of keys across the speaker.

"Hmm. The units are selling pretty fast. I can send you a link to the virtual tour so you can see for yourselves what the condos will look like when they're finished," Pepe said, and the sounds of the keys followed again and then a bing to confirm the email had arrived.

"Thanks, Pepe. I know you usually like to stay out of things—"

"I do. Stay safe," Pepe said and hung up.

Mariela had sensed the undertones as the men had finished the call. She narrowed her eyes to peer at Ricky as he opened the email and brought up the virtual tour on the large television screen on the far wall.

"I get the sense Pepe didn't want to be involved in this," Mariela said, once again feeling guilty about bringing yet another family member into the mess of her life.

Ricky did an uneasy shrug. "Pepe tries to shy away from South Beach Security. He's made his own success as a real estate agent."

"It must not be easy to be the next generation in a family like yours," she said, aware of some of the history of the family.

The shrug greeted her again, which she was learning meant he was uncomfortable with the discussion. "I don't mean to pry," she said and gestured toward the laptop as a way to shift the conversation away from the family dynamics.

Ricky met her gaze head-on, clearly aware of what she was trying to do. "How about I share if you share?"

MARIELA OPENED HER eyes wide and her voice almost squeaked as she said, "Share?"

Ricky nodded. "Yes, share. Like why it's hard for me and Pepe to be the next generation and why you dropped out of college."

A very visible gulp from Mariela warned it might be difficult for her to start the share, so he began. "My *abuelo*, *papi*, his brother Jose and Trey were all military. Heroes who came home and became even larger than life after. *Abuelo* started the agency and *papi* has kept it going."

"And now Trey is here to continue the legacy," Mariela finished for him.

Ricky dipped his head to confirm it. "Trey is the natural successor. I may help out on occasion, but my dream is to build my practice. What about you?"

Mariela hesitated and looked away, avoiding his gaze, and despite how open he'd been, he realized she wasn't quite ready to tell her life story. He didn't press. She'd share when she was ready.

"Let's take a look at the condo units," he said after her obvious hesitation and opened the link Pepe had sent.

Together they did a virtual walk-through of what the various condos would look like when they were finished.

As much as Ricky didn't like Jorge based on how he had abused Mariela, he had to admit that the condos looked great on the virtual tour. He could understand why the units were selling fast.

But despite that, something niggled in the back of his brain.

"Do you think this is the place you overheard Jorge discussing?"

Mariela worried her lower lip as she considered his question. "Possibly. I mean, this is his biggest new project."

Big and costly, Ricky thought, but didn't want to jump to any conclusions because too much was at stake.

"Let's take a look at the other new construction and finish going through the list," he said.

They reviewed the other pending projects, a mid-rise condo of one hundred units near the beach and a subdevelopment of half a dozen custom homes farther inland. The first would certainly make Mariela's ex a few million. The homes less because of their size and the neighborhood.

After, they scrutinized the list of completed projects over the last few years, marking up those that Mariela remembered had had issues that suddenly went away.

Jorge had been quite busy until this year, Ricky thought, and Mariela had noticed the same thing.

"He hasn't done as many projects since the divorce, but then again, that high-rise is costly," Mariela said, but Ricky detected something in her tone.

"You shouldn't feel guilty," he said, imagining

that she felt the divorce was somehow responsible for the issues Jorge might be having.

With a shrug of her shoulders, she said, "I shouldn't feel guilty, but I do. Maybe the settlement I got—"

"Which you deserved for all the work you did for him. Maybe his business isn't doing well because he's missing your wonderful events and marketing," Ricky said.

MARIELA CONSIDERED HIS words and they filled her with warmth. "I did do a lot of good work for him," she said with a determined nod.

"You did," he said and gestured to the list they had marked up. "We can wait until Sophie and Robbie look up the inspectors, but we can also get started ourselves," he said and immediately worked on the computer to create an account in the building inspection department's online portal to review the reports for the various projects she had identified.

They were about to search the records for the first location when Samantha sashayed into the room and over to the table. "How is it going?" she asked, laying a hand on Ricky's shoulder in a very maternal gesture.

"Good, but if you're here, I'm gathering you need us for something," Ricky said, totally in tune with his mother.

"I do, *mi'jo*. You obviously haven't noticed that

it's time for dinner," she said. She stroked her hand across his back and winced again as Ricky looked up at her and she noticed the bruises on his face.

"*Gracias, mami.* We'll be there soon," Ricky said, obvious affection in his voice.

"Not too long. Your siblings, Roni and Carolina are already here. So are your *abuelos*," she said and hurried away.

Mariela's stomach clenched with a sick feeling at the thought of meeting his grandparents as well as trying to be social with the other Gonzalez family members.

"It'll be okay. They don't bite, although Mia and Carolina can be a little over the top," Ricky said with a smile and a small grimace.

She didn't worry about the Twins since she knew them relatively well and had seen them the day before. But the reception from Ricky's grandparents was an unknown, especially considering all that had happened in the last twenty-four hours. If it were her family, she wouldn't be very pleased with the person who had brought danger to them.

Sucking in a deep, bracing breath, she accepted the hand Ricky offered and rose from the table. He didn't release her hand, gently guiding her toward the back of the home and a large outdoor dining area with an immense glass and wrought-iron table.

The rest of the family was already seated there and stood as Ricky and she walked in.

She tensed and Ricky squeezed her hand in reassurance. "Mariela, say hello to the family."

Chapter Nine

An older man walked over, followed by a small almost birdlike woman, and held out his hand. "Mariela. Ramon Gonzalez," he said and grasped her hand warmly in his two big hands. "My wife, Maria."

The woman also shook Mariela's hand with affection, relieving some of her apprehension about meeting them.

"Mis abuelos," Ricky said, although she had guessed that already. It was obvious the younger Gonzalez family members got their Roman noses and dimpled chins from their grandfather. The brilliant blues of their eyes had come from Maria. His grandparents had to be in their late eighties, but there was nothing about them that hinted at that age. They moved with grace and assurance.

His grandfather swept a hand in the direction of the family gathered around the table. "You've already met the rest of the family, I gather. *Ramoncito* and his wife, Samantha. My grandson Ramon the third. It's why we call him Trey. His fiancée, Roni. My granddaughters Mia and Carolina."

Mariela did an awkward little wave at the remaining family members before Ricky slipped a hand to her back and guided her to the two empty seats at the table.

A second later a woman who looked like an older version of Josie wheeled in a serving cart with several large platters and placed it off to one side of the covered dining area. Josie and another man followed with smaller platters, placed them on a side table and began serving the food.

As they did so, Ricky said, "This is Josie's mom, Alicia. The young man is Javier, their cousin."

A family affair, Mariela thought, and as the three served those at the table, it was apparent there was real affection between the two families despite their different stations in life.

The appetizer consisted of a play on a tamale, with a light and fluffy corn meal base topped with *picadillo* and *cotija* cheese.

Appreciative murmurs filled the air as everyone tried the dish and Mariela had to agree. The sharp taste of the *picadillo* with its tomato sauce and ground meat was balanced perfectly by the sweetness of the corn meal and saltiness of the cheese.

"You outdid yourself, Alicia," Ricky said after

he'd finished his food and Alicia and her family prepped the dishes with the main meal.

To her surprise, Trey, Mia and Ricky got up from the table to help clear off the dishes while plates piled high with *arroz con pollo* and sweet plantains were served to everyone.

She hadn't been hungry at first, too worried and caught up in all that they were trying to investigate, but the delicious tamale pie as well as the feelings of warmth and friendliness around the table had awakened her appetite.

Once the siblings had sat again, the family started eating and chatting about everything except what had happened the night before and that morning. She appreciated their thoughtfulness and got so swept up in that sense of normal she almost forgot why she was sitting there at the table.

Almost being the operative word, especially as she caught sight of the armed guards down at the waterfront, patrolling the dock area.

When tension crept into her body, Ricky immediately swept a hand up her back to offer a calming stroke. It surprised her that she didn't recoil the way she often did when a man came by, but then again Ricky had shown her he was anything but an ordinary man.

The siblings once again got up to help Alicia and her family clean up so that coffee and flan could be set out for dessert.

She had thought she was full, but it was impossible not to finish the wonderfully prepared flan Josie placed in front of her.

Once they'd finished, Ricky leaned close and said, "What about a walk?"

Mariela really wanted to get back to work on reviewing the lists and hesitated, but Ricky said, "It'll clear our minds so we can be more efficient."

He was hard to refuse, especially as he grinned, which made him look boyish despite the bruises on his face.

She nodded, and he rose and said, "If you'll excuse us. We're going to get some air."

"Of course. We'll have some more coffee," his grandfather said, but Mariela sensed the family would be doing more than just having coffee.

She forced those thoughts away to allow herself to enjoy the last rays of the sun as dusk fled and was replaced by night.

Ricky guided her toward the water's edge where the security guards had drifted away to either end of the property, giving them some privacy.

Water lapped up against the bulkhead at the edge of the yard and the hull of the speedboat docked there. Across the canal and causeway were the lights in the port and the skyline of Miami snapping to life at night. Even farther in the distance, the final kiss of sunlight bathed the waters of Biscayne Bay with shades of pink, purple and blue.

A light breeze swept off the water, rustling the fronds of the palms above them.

"Beautiful," she said, appreciating how the man-made elements blended with those of nature to create the stunning scene playing out before them.

"It is," Ricky said, a hint of something in his tone that dragged her attention to him.

He was gazing at her with the kind of interest she hadn't seen in a long time. Or maybe it was better to say what she had avoided for a long time. And which she wanted to avoid what with all that was going on.

"It's too soon," she said, and he smiled sadly and nodded.

"I understand."

They turned back toward the house, their pace slow. A calm silence settled over them as they enjoyed those last few moments of daylight and the peace before reality intruded again.

HIS FAMILY WAS huddled together at the table.

Ricky had no doubt what they were talking about. He tempered his anger that they hadn't included him because he knew they were only trying to do what they thought was best. Even Roni was in on the family discussion despite the fact that Trey and she had only recently become engaged.

Normally he was only tangentially involved in

their investigations, offering his opinions on their possible suspects or counseling their clients.

But he thought he had proved in the last twenty-four hours that he could be more, do more, as part of South Beach Security.

As Mariela and he approached the table, Trey gestured for them to join the discussion. "We didn't mean to exclude you," Trey said, as if reading his thoughts.

"I'm up for this," he said, determined to be in control of his fate during this investigation.

"We know," Mia and Carolina said, almost in unison.

"Please sit," his father suggested, but before he could, his grandparents rose from the table.

"You'll have to excuse us. We'd like to get home before it gets too late," his *abuelo* said and helped his grandmother stand, offering his arm in a gallant gesture.

Ricky walked over to hug them, grateful they had come to visit, although it had likely been to confirm that he was okay after all that had happened in the last day.

When his grandparents stepped away from the table, his grandfather faced Mariela. "It was very nice to meet you. I promise we'll take care of you," he said.

"I know you will," she said with a smile, but Ricky couldn't miss that her smile was stilted, and she had wrapped her arms around herself again, clearly in defensive mode.

His grandfather peered at the rest of the family. "You'll call if you need me," he said, and Ramon and Trey nodded.

"We will," Ricky's father said, and with that his grandparents slowly ambled off, arm in arm. Their heads bent together as they chatted while they walked.

It brought a little ache in his heart to see them so in love after over sixty years of marriage and because he had always hoped that he'd have the same kind of love one day. Which made him shoot a quick peek at Mariela, who still stood there uneasily.

Slipping his hand to her back, he urged her to the table so they could sit and discuss the investigation.

His butt had no sooner hit the seat when Trey said, "Roni was just telling us that she heard back from some other detectives who had experienced issues with Mariela's DA."

Mariela plucked at the tablecloth nervously. "What did they say?"

Roni did a little shake of her head and her lips tightened. "Mariela's case isn't unique, unfortunately. This DA supports no bail for offenders, even violent ones. He's also using extreme discretion as to what crimes to prosecute."

"If I understand you correctly, it's possible

Jorge and his attorney had nothing to do with the DA not charging him," Mariela said with another, more violent tug at the tablecloth, which she then smoothed with shaky hands.

He laid an arm across her shoulders, and she did a little flinch but then relaxed with his touch.

"That's very possible," Roni said with a frustrated sigh. "It makes our jobs harder and decreases public safety, but what can you do?"

"How about speaking to Jose? He is one of the senior DAs," his mother said and glanced at her husband, who had a close relationship with his brother.

"I will. A prosecutor is responsible for protecting the community and people like Mariela. That didn't happen," Ramon said.

"It didn't. The detectives were also able to pull the video from Ricky's security system and from some of your neighbors' doorbell cameras. Hopefully they can get some useful photos of the suspect and the car," Roni advised.

"Did you two find anything useful?" Trey asked.

Ricky and Mariela shared a look. "We reviewed Hernandez's new construction projects. Two of them could generate a lot of money for him. We also have a list of his older construction jobs and were just going to start reviewing the inspection reports on those," he said.

"Do you need help?" Trey asked.

"Sophie and Robbie are going to help. Once we have a list of the inspectors, we can decide what to do," he said.

"I'll try to remember which of the inspectors are ones I remember from Jorge's work," Mariela added.

"Roni and I will stay on top of the detectives investigating your assault and the shooting. Hopefully they'll have something that will help us with what we're doing," Trey said and slapped the tabletop as if to signal that their discussion was done. That was confirmed as he stood and held out a hand to his fiancée.

Roni slipped her hand into his but glanced their way. "We will keep on top of this."

"We know you will," his mother said and likewise rose from the table.

Since it was obviously time to go, he stood and Mariela joined him, slipping her hand into his as they followed his family back into the house.

He took comfort from the fact that Mariela had made that first small move. It spoke of a growing trust between them and that she was possibly beginning to heal from the trauma of her abusive marriage.

Inside, the couples all shared goodbyes before Trey and Roni left to go home, and his parents went upstairs to their wing of the house.

"Are you game to keep on working?" Ricky

asked, unsure of whether Mariela was up to it after all the events of the night before and that morning.

She nodded. "I am. I'd like to get to the bottom of this as soon as we can."

So she could be back to her regular life, he thought. *Hopefully one without fear.*

In his father's study they sat back at the table and split the list into three to speed their review. They sent one third to Sophie and Robbie so they could make their list of the inspectors on the projects. Mariela and he took the other sections and got to work.

As MARIELA READ through the inspection reports, she tried to recall some of the conversations she'd overheard over the years, and which had roused suspicions in her that Jorge might be doing something shady. When they'd first been married and she'd started helping him with the business, she'd asked him about what was happening.

That had been the first time she'd seen the monster emerge in Jorge and the memory actually made her stomach twist with fear.

She should have seen the signs then. The quick, explosive anger. The name-calling.

She'd written it off as Jorge being under pressure to build his business and possible money issues, but over time that monster would materialize more and more often. At first it had been verbal, and then it had become physical. A slap across the face. A punch to the stomach.

The beating that had landed her in the hospital when she'd asked him about some unusual expenses. One of the business's accountants had questioned why one of her events had been so costly, only she hadn't spent anything near that amount the accountant had mentioned.

Which made her say, "Jorge used to hide some expenses by charging them to things like the promotions he asked me to do."

Ricky looked up from his laptop. "You think he used that money to pay people off?"

Remembering his anger when she'd questioned him, she now had no doubt that's what he was doing. "I think so. I just don't know how to prove it."

Ricky leaned back in his chair, steepled his arms on the edges and tapped his mouth with his fingers as he considered what she'd said. "Did he give you any financial information when you were trying to get divorced?"

The financial settlement had been something they'd fought about repeatedly. As part of that process, her ex's attorneys had sent info, but her attorney and his experts had been the ones to look at it.

"My attorney has that info. I could ask him for it, only I don't know how detailed it is," she said. She logged into her email account and instantly sent a request for the information.

"If it is detailed, it may help us identify if and when bribes occurred," Ricky said and returned to the perusal of his list.

She did the same, but soon the reports were forming a jumble in her brain and her eyes were drifting closed.

Not good, she thought and shot a peek at Ricky. He leaned forward in his chair, his attention squarely on the information on the screen. Every now and then he'd jot something down on the list and on a pad of paper beside him, much like she had done as she reviewed her entries.

He seemed alert enough. Even though it was imperative that they get to the bottom of what was happening, she didn't want to possibly miss something important because she was tired.

Ricky must have sensed her distraction. He looked her way and said, "I can see you need to rest."

"I do. I'm a little tired," she admitted. In the past she would have kept something like that secret, afraid of the retribution if she didn't do what Jorge wanted.

"I am, too. Let's call it a night," he said and shut his laptop.

"Thanks," she said, appreciating his understanding.

He sighed, pushed out of the leather chair and stood before her. His gaze was intense as he looked at her and said, "You never have to hesitate with me, Mariela."

Inside she knew that somehow, but it didn't make it to her brain as she said, "I need time to learn to trust, Ricky."

"I KNOW. BELIEVE ME, I know," Ricky said. It was his job to understand as a professional, but even though their relationship had started that way, it had definitely morphed into something more personal with all that was happening.

But he didn't press.

He gave her space as she left the table, walked out into the living area and up the stairs to the guest wing. At her door, she laid a hand on the jamb and faced him. "I don't know how to thank you for everything you and your family are doing."

"It's what we do," he said and once again realized that he was as much a part of SBS as the three Ramons, his grandmother and mother, the Twins and his tech-savvy cousins.

She cupped his cheek, tenderly stroked her thumb across his evening stubble, mindful of the bruises, and smiled, a real smile that made her emerald-colored eyes sparkle with bits of lighter green and blue. "Good night."

He stroked his hand over hers and grinned. "Good night," he said and waited until she had closed her door behind her. But he didn't head to his bedroom right away.

Lightly treading down the stairs, he went to do a walk around the grounds to make sure all was in order.

Chapter Ten

It shouldn't have surprised him that he ran into his father by the front door.

"*Mi'jo*. There was no need for you to come down," his father said.

He smiled and clapped his father on the back. "I can say the same about you, *papi*."

"Let's walk," he said with a half smile, and they strolled out the door together and to the front gate, which was firmly locked.

As they did their tour of the grounds, his father said, "Mariela seems like an interesting woman."

He wasn't quite sure what to make of his father's use of "interesting."

"She's had a hard time in her life recently," he said in her defense.

His father raised his hand. "I understand she's been abused, *mi'jo*. I'm just concerned about what that means for our family, especially you."

"Because I'm not like *abuelo* or you or Trey," he said, feeling that insecurity that he had battled for so much of his life rise to the surface.

A rough laugh escaped his father. "We might be physically stronger, but what you have in here..." he said and tapped a spot in the center of Ricky's chest. "What you have there is as strong. Maybe stronger."

He was so shocked he didn't know what to say. Instead, he ambled beside his father in the quiet of the night, making sure their home was safe and secure. They strolled around the perimeter of the lot and down to the dock. Bright moonlight illuminated the waters of the bay and canal. A row of lights along the top edge of the bulkhead snapped to life and made the two guards at either end of the property visible.

At the wave of his father's hand, they walked over to join them.

"Everything okay, Esteban? Patrick?"

"All is in order, *jefe*," Esteban said and gestured toward the canal. "No one will get past us."

"Thank you," Ricky said and looked toward the canal. With the moonlight and the lights along the water's edge, any approach would be way too visible. But that morning's attack in broad daylight had been pretty brazen also.

When the guards returned to their positions and his father and he sauntered toward the house, he said, "I want to be ready to defend us."

His father stopped short and peered at him in the dim light beneath a stand of palm trees. A slight breeze shifted the palms, making the fronds crackle and snap.

"I know you're familiar with using a gun. I didn't think you liked them," his father said.

"I don't, but there's a time for everything and I think it's time," he admitted, trusting that the training he'd received over the years would serve him well. Certainly, the martial arts instruction had the night before.

His father laid an arm across his shoulders. "Come with me."

They hurried into the house where his father armed the security system and led him back into his study. At the far end of the room, his father reached into a panel on one of the built-ins and the section swung open like a door: the entrance to the gun range and the small armory beneath the first floor.

They entered the narrow staircase and Ricky closed the door behind them. It had been years since he'd been down in the basement. When they were younger his father would regularly take him and his siblings there so they could learn how to shoot and handle a weapon.

His father had always said that you needed to be prepared to defend your country. As he did so, he'd tell them stories of fleeing Cuba and how his father, their *abuelo*, had fought to make Cuba free. Often, he also shared his stories of being in the marines and serving overseas and then as a police officer.

Ricky had listened and watched. He had even taken his turns shooting when it was time, not that he enjoyed it. But as he'd just told his father, he understood there might be a time when you needed to use a gun.

He stood by his father as he used his palm to open the biometric lock on a large gun safe near the base of the hidden staircase.

Ricky helped him open the heavy doors to reveal half a dozen or so rifles, some of them semi-automatic. Two shotguns. Half a dozen pistols, both semis and revolvers.

He drifted his fingers over the weapons and picked up a nine-millimeter Glock. He checked to make sure there wasn't a bullet in the chamber, not that his father would store a weapon that way, but you always had to check.

"Do you want to reacquaint yourself with it?" his father asked and grabbed a smaller twenty-two-caliber Smith and Wesson from the safe.

The gun range was soundproofed. No one above them would hear a thing if he decided to shoot off a few rounds and test his skills.

He nodded. It had been a few years since he'd fired a weapon. If he needed to use the gun, he wanted to be prepared. Grabbing a magazine and box of ammo, he slipped on protective glasses and ear protection and walked to one of the lanes in the range.

There was a pad with paper targets hanging on one wall and he ripped one off and placed it on the target carrier. With the push of a button, he moved the target down the lane about twenty-five feet.

Carefully he loaded the magazine, slammed it into the grip of the gun, pulled back the slide and flipped the safety off.

His father came up behind him to watch as Ricky took aim and fired. He emptied the entire magazine and was pleased to see that most of the bullets had hit center mass on the target. He removed the magazine, engaged the safety, reloaded and fired off another round of bullets. This time he aimed for different areas on the target and, when he was finished, smiled in satisfaction at hitting his mark almost every time.

With a woot, his father heartily clapped his back. "You haven't lost your touch. You could give Mia a run for the money."

He slipped the magazine from the gun, flipped on the safety and laid the gun on the tabletop. Removing his ear protection, he said in a puzzled tone, "I could give *Mia* a run?"

"Your sister has become quite the shot. Better than Trey. By the way, I've kept your concealed carry permit in order if you want to take that one," he said and gestured to the Glock.

Ricky hesitated and looked from the gun to the

target. With a nod, he said, "I'll take it. Are you going to use that one?"

His father shook his head. "No stopping power." He reached behind him, lifted the hem of his *guayabera* shirt and withdrew his gun to show to Ricky. It was an old-style Dirty Harry revolver and loaded. "Never jams."

"I'll keep that in mind," he said, but he'd bet on his fifteen bullets over his father's seven any day. He returned to the tabletop, loaded the magazine and slipped it into the gun. He made sure the safety was on, and when his father handed him a holster, he secured the gun in it and tucked the holster in his waistband against the small of his back.

The weight of it felt weird there. Totally foreign because it was out of his wheelhouse. But given all that had happened last night and this morning, he intended to be prepared for the next time even though he prayed there wouldn't be a next time.

He hoped that the detectives on the two cases would get some useful evidence from the crime scenes and the videos they had gathered to help identify their suspect.

Armed with that hope, he walked back up to the main floor with his father. They embraced in the foyer and his father tightened his hold and said, "I'm very proud of the man you've become."

The words meant more than his father could imagine. For too long he'd lived in the shadow of the three Ramons and even the Twins. All unique and amazing individuals, which was why he'd always felt more comfortable with his more subdued techie cousins and Pepe, who avoided South Beach Security involvement at all costs.

"Good night, *papi*. I love you," he said. His father had always been a good father. Kind. Patient. Supportive. Loving. The insecurities about who he was in the family dynamic had been ones he'd inserted into their relationship, he realized.

His father playfully ruffled his hair and smiled. "I love you, too, *mi' jo*. Get some rest. Tomorrow will be a busy day."

With a nod, he hurried up the stairs, taking them two at a time in his rush to get to his bedroom, but he skidded to a halt at the sight of Mariela's closed door.

His heart told him to check in on her, but his brain said it was best to leave her alone.

It was much too soon for anyone to handle such new feelings and even harder for someone as fragile as Mariela. He had seen how defensive she'd been during her short stint in the support group as well as her initial reactions to his touch and nearness.

She needed the time alone to process what was happening and realize she wasn't alone anymore.

She had the police, his family and him to watch her back.

Much like he'd risen to the challenges presented recently, now it was time for her to harness the inner strength he'd seen to overcome the hurt of the past and build her future.

With that in mind, he turned away from her door and went to his room to get some rest and prepare for tomorrow and the challenges it would bring.

"I PAID YOU to scare her off, not shoot up houses," Jorge shouted and ran a hand through his hair in frustration. "And why didn't you pick up last night? I must have called a dozen times."

"I was trying to lay low, and it wasn't me who shot at them," his former foreman said. He had fired the man for coming to work drunk one time too many, and it was obvious now that he shouldn't have relied on him to do any kind of job. He was sure the man was lying about trying to shoot Mariela.

He paced back and forth across his living room, his fist tight around his cell phone as he said, "All you had to do was warn her to keep her mouth shut."

"I didn't get a chance," the man whined. "She had some guy with her who came in like a ninja or something."

Ninja, Jorge thought and scoffed. His old foreman had probably been drunk again when he'd gone to Mariela's. Maybe even when he'd decided to shoot up the house in Gables by the Sea.

"You royally messed this up. I need you to disappear for a while," Jorge said, his gut twisting with fear at what would happen if anyone discovered he'd paid for the attack.

"What's a while? I can't afford to just up and take a vacation. I need more money," his foreman said.

With what he'd already paid the idiot he could take quite a lot of time off. But he had something different in mind for his former employee.

"Do you know where my new high-rise is going up?"

At the man's grunt, he said, "Meet me there at midnight tonight. I'll have more money for you."

"Thanks, *jefe*," the man said and hung up.

Jorge stopped pacing and paused by the wall of windows that faced the perfectly landscaped gardens surrounding his very expensive pool and spa. Turning, he scrutinized the modern and lavish furniture in the living room and, beyond that, the dream designer kitchen.

He didn't know any woman who wouldn't have wanted to live in such luxury.

Except Mariela, of course.

It hadn't been like that at first. They'd been happy. But Mariela hadn't understood the pressures he'd been under. Hadn't appreciated that everything he'd been doing had been for her.

Always for her, but no longer. Now he had to put himself first.

BY LATE MORNING the next day they had made a list of building inspectors who had handled the various projects Mariela had identified as being problematic. They had also noted a pattern in those projects and others where the two inspectors would reinspect items that had previously failed. Miraculously the buildings would then pass inspection.

Some of those second inspections happened to match up with some odd expenses in the financial statements her attorney had sent over earlier. Much like Mariela had thought, her ex had been hiding the payoffs by claiming them as the costs for marketing and other promotions.

"I remember that there were a few complaints about this building," Mariela said and ran a finger across the one entry on their list.

Ricky nodded. "Maybe there are more at these other buildings as well. Even lawsuits, if the situation is bad enough. We could do a search of the court records for those."

"There was at least one, I think," Mariela confirmed and screwed her eyes shut as she attempted to recall. She popped her eyes open when she remembered and jabbed at another entry on their list of suspect properties. "This one, I think."

"Good job. Let's call Sophie and Robbie to see what they have and if they can help us get the court records," Ricky said.

He speed-dialed his cousins, who immediately answered. "Good morning, Ricky. We were just about to send our analysis of the list you sent. Lots of hinky things there," Sophie said.

"I've got you on speaker, Soph. We've got suspicious things as well. We were hoping you could help us get information on any lawsuits filed against Hernandez's company," Ricky advised.

"We can. How about information on these building inspectors?" Robbie asked.

Ricky took a quick look at her, as if seeking confirmation, and she nodded. "It might help us decide if they're taking bribes," she said.

With a quick dip of his head, he said, "What kind of info can you get?"

"You'd be surprised what's available publicly and what people share," Sophie said with a husky laugh.

Mariela didn't doubt it. She was often shocked by the kind of information people posted on social media. "Whatever you can get would be great," she said.

"We'll touch base with you later. In the meantime, you might want to discuss this information with *Tia* Elena and see what she thinks," Robbie added and ended the call.

A ding immediately followed to advise that an email had arrived. Ricky opened it and printed out the list from his cousins. As they examined it, the same two names that were on their list kept popping up.

"Do you think your aunt can do something with this information?" Mariela asked, doubting that they had enough at the moment for any kind of criminal charges against the men.

"Maybe not, but if she thinks we're on to something, she probably knows who to contact," he said and dialed his aunt.

The conversation with her was short and hopeful since Elena felt there might be enough there to reach out to authorities who could decide whether to investigate the two men.

"That's great, *tia*. We'll get together everything we have and send it to you shortly," Ricky said and hung up.

"What do we do now?" Mariela worried that they had to do more so life could go back to normal. Whatever normal was. She hadn't had normal in a long time. Maybe it would be possible one day, and as she met Ricky's bright blue-eyed gaze, hope grew within her that it would happen soon.

Chapter Eleven

Ricky powered up the engines of the speedboat and pulled away from the dock, Mariela in the cockpit beside him. They'd left the security guards on land to protect his parents, although he was certain his father could handle the kind of trouble likely to come his way. Especially with the discussion he'd had with his father and Trey just a few minutes before while Mariela and his mother had been cleaning up from lunch.

Both his father and brother were certain that it was a one-man operation trying to take out Mariela and probably not a professional. If it had been a professional Mariela would have likely been killed during the first attack. As for the shooting, Trey had been told that the police had a partial license plate number from one of the neighbors' doorbell video feeds. A professional would have been more careful and blacked out the license plate.

Armed with that knowledge, it seemed reasonable to take the boat out to one of the building locations they had identified the night before. He hoped that a quick visual inspection might give them a clue if something was going on with it.

The high-rise condo under construction was located near Bal Harbour and it wouldn't take long to drive the boat to that area.

"Are you sure we'll be okay?" Mariela said, peering around the area as he turned out of the canal and into the waters of Biscayne Bay.

Guilt filled him that he hadn't shared that afternoon's report. "I'm sorry I didn't tell you before. There's been some progress on the case," he said and relayed the information he had discussed with Trey and his father.

"That's good news," she said, visibly relaxing in her seat.

"It is. Hopefully with that info and what we sent to *Tia* Elena, we'll be able to make more progress and keep you safe," he said, steering across the bay and toward the northern-most points on Miami Beach.

"Safe," she said with a harsh laugh.

From the corner of his eye, he could see her retreating again as she wrapped her arms around herself.

"I know it's hard for you to believe that. You haven't been safe in a long time," he said and laid his hand on the throttle, preparing to give the engines some speed. "You strapped in well?"

She pulled on the seat belt straps and, seemingly satisfied, nodded.

"Hold on," he said and pushed the throttle forward, increasing the speed slowly at first, but once they were safely between the mainland and Miami Beach, he pushed the boat to its top speed.

They flew over the surface, water splashing over the bow and windshield as they hit a small swell. The spray drenched them, and he laughed, feeling more carefree than he had in a long time. Her laughter drifted over to him as well and he was grateful that she was enjoying the ride.

He zigged and zagged, mindful of other boats in the area, sending more water up and over. Enjoying Mariela's delight with the ride until they got closer to the location of her ex's new development. He slowed the boat's speed until they neared the backside of the construction site where he killed the boat's engine and pulled out a pair of binoculars to examine the location.

As the boat rocked from a passing wake, Mariela bumped into him.

He slipped an arm around her waist to steady her and handed her the binoculars.

"I don't see anything out of the ordinary," he said as she took them and brought them up to her eyes.

"Not many people working today. Usually there's more activity on a project of this size," she said and gestured to the very bare bones of the building.

At his questioning gaze, she said, "You pick

up a few things when you work on projects like this." She motioned to the location again. "Could you get a little closer?"

"Sure. Strap yourself in again," he said and, as soon as she was secured, he cut into the channel of water between Bay Harbour and Bal Harbour so they could get a close-up look at the structure. From what he could see, maybe two dozen men or so were ambling around the property doing a lot of nothing.

"Is that typical?" he asked, wondering how anything got built with so few men and such little labor going on.

MARIELA RAISED THE binoculars and surveyed the construction location. He was right that it was far from typical. She'd been on many a job site to show investors around and they'd always been a hub of activity. "It's not," she said and zoomed in to look at where a number of workers sat on a large pile of steel beams, playing a game of cards.

"It looks like they've driven the steel piles for securing the foundation. That usually means they'd be pouring concrete by now," she explained and handed Ricky the binoculars.

He was about to raise them when the windshield of the speedboat suddenly cracked, and a Sea-Doo raced past them. The rider turned, his face mostly hidden by the cowl of the wetsuit he wore, and fired at them again, shattering another section on the windshield.

Mariela ducked down, but Ricky whipped out a gun and opened fire on the Sea-Doo. The rider must have thought better of attacking again and sped away from them, bouncing across the waves created by the wake of a passing boat.

"HANG ON," RICKY SAID, whipped their boat around and chased after the Sea-Doo, catching up to it easily with the greater power of the speedboat.

Ricky stayed on the tail of the Sea-Doo, trying to get a better look at the rider, but as the Sea-Doo turned toward land, Ricky had to slow down and then stop. The large outboard engines, which had given him the speed to catch up to their shooter, prevented him from entering the shallower waters.

He banged his hand in frustration against the steering wheel and cursed. "He got away. Are you okay?"

"Bounced around a little, but okay otherwise," she said.

"We need to head back, but first…" He whipped out his phone and dialed Trey. When his brother answered, he said, "We were attacked again. Rider on a Sea-Doo. He was headed toward the eastern side of Bal Harbour the last time I saw him."

"How do you know it's a 'him'?" Trey asked.

"Too big and bulky for a woman. He had the same build as the person who shot at us yesterday," he said, recalling what he'd seen of the watercraft rider and yesterday's attacker.

"I'll call some friends on the force there and have them ask around at the local marinas. He has to pull in somewhere," Trey said.

"Thanks. We're headed back to the house," he said, but plopped into the captain's chair as his knees suddenly felt weak.

"Are you sure you're okay?" Mariela asked and laid a hand on his chest, directly above his heart.

He took hold of her hand and brought it to his lips. "I'm fine. Just a little shaken, as I imagine you are."

"I am. I'll be better once we're home," she said with a smile.

Home. The word sounded nice coming off her lips. Those full lips that he'd thought about last night as he'd finally drifted off to sleep. He found himself shifting toward her, closer and closer to those lips he wanted to taste until the rev of an engine reminded him they weren't safe out here on open water.

He stroked a hand across her cheek, trailing his thumb along the line of her lips. "Let's go home."

HIS MOTHER WAS waiting for them back at the house, nervously pacing back and forth along the length of the dock. Hands tucked beneath her arms. She stopped at the sight of the speedboat, hurried to the water's edge and grabbed hold of the line that Mariela tossed to her while he eased the boat closer.

One of the security guards rushed over to tie the line onto a cleat while the second man stood to secure the area and protect them.

He killed the engine as Mariela tossed out a second line and he rushed over to make sure the bumpers were in place. Once the boat was tied to the dock, he jumped out onto the wooden planks and helped Mariela from the boat.

His mother's blue-eyed gaze, so much like his own, mirrored his worry. He forced a smile to his lips, trying to dispel her fear. "I handled it."

She shook her head and tears glistened in her eyes. "I know. It's just that I hoped... I was glad when you didn't join the agency because it meant you were safe. Now..."

"It will be fine. Trey is already working on getting more information for us," he said, reassuring his mother.

She nodded and abruptly rushed toward the house.

He sighed and Mariela slipped her arm around his waist. "She's just worried."

"Who isn't?" he said and mimicked Mariela's gesture, encircling her waist with his arm and drawing her close. "Let's get cleaned up. I'm sure Trey and *papi* will be here soon and want a report on what happened."

"Then let's get going," she said, and they

walked arm in arm toward the house, hips bumping. They didn't separate once inside and went up the stairs together. In the small foyer before their bedrooms, they finally parted to stand there and stare at each other.

Ricky cupped her cheek and stepped close until her warm breath spilled against his lips. Soft and regular at first, but then harder, faster, when he laid a hand at her waist and closed the gap between them.

She inched up on tiptoes and met his lips with hers, the kiss gentle. Hesitant as if she hadn't kissed anyone in a long time.

He didn't press, aware of her past. Hoping to build trust for the future.

He let her end the kiss, giving her the control she'd lacked in her life for so long.

When she stepped away, he ran the back of his hand across her cheek. "I'll meet you downstairs when you're done."

MARIELA COULDN'T FIND her voice. Her throat was too choked up with the emotion of that so simple, but so pure, touch.

All she could do was nod and rush off to her bedroom to wash off the sea spray from their ride and the fear that had gripped her yet again at the sound of the first bullet hitting the boat's windshield.

He had defended her again, risking his life. Again.

She had no doubt it was going to happen again. This time she intended to be prepared for it just like Ricky had been prepared. She'd been surprised when he'd pulled out a weapon to chase away their attacker, but he'd handled it with ease.

After their meeting with Trey and his father, she was going to ask Ricky to show her how to protect herself. She wouldn't be caught defenseless again.

"ARE YOU SURE you want to do this?" Ricky asked, worry slithering through him even as he slipped off his shoes and stepped onto the mat in the family gym.

"I want to be able to do something," Mariela said and toed off her sneakers. She grabbed the loose strands of her caramel-colored hair and did a little flip and twist with it that turned the longish strands into a top knot. An oversize T-shirt with the U of M logo hung loosely over her upper body and the leggings she had changed into after dinner and a short walk around the grounds. As they had strolled to the water's edge, she had asked him to teach her how to defend herself.

She stepped onto the mat, and he shook his head with doubt but began the lesson. "Okay. Let's start with what to do if someone grabs you from behind," he said and took a position at her back, his arm wrapped around her throat.

"First thing to do is to jam your elbow into their midsection," he said and instructed her to mimic the action. When she did, he play-acted the position he'd be in, doubled over slightly and said, "Now you can either use your elbow or the palm of your hand to hit them in the nose."

She tried to do it but couldn't quite come around because of their height difference. "I can't," she said, dejection in her voice.

"That's okay. If you can't, drive your foot into his instep, especially if you've got heels on," he instructed.

She made believe she had done that, and Ricky released her so that they were now facing one another. "Now that you're free, use your legs. Women's legs are their strongest feature. Kick him in the groin. The knee. Anywhere, really."

Mariela hesitated, clearly not wanting to hurt him. "I get it."

Ricky nodded. "Once he's doubled over, don't stop. Use the heel of your palm and smash his nose in or punch him in the throat."

"And after that?" she asked.

"Scream. Actually, start screaming the moment he grabs you. If that doesn't scare him off, someone may hear and call the police. If you have keys in your hand, put them between your fingers and jab at his eyes or throat. Anything to disable the person," he said and was about to show her another move when his cell phone started ringing.

"It's Trey," he said and put the phone on speaker.

"I have good news and bad news. Which do you want to hear first?" Trey said.

Ricky met Mariela's worry-filled gaze. "The bad news," she said.

"They tracked down the license plate on the BMW, but it appears to have been stolen."

Ricky muttered a curse and shook his head. "Is that all the bad news?"

"Yes. The good news is we have more video of the car from a marina in Bal Harbour. Probably stolen plates again, but we were able to confirm the make and model of the car. It's a late model black BMW 330 sedan."

With a low whistle, Ricky said, "There must be thousands of them in the Miami-Dade area."

"There are, but the vehicle had some distinguishing features—a custom spoiler and front bumper valance. There was also a decal on a side window that looks like it's from a local university."

"I guess that's good news," Mariela said, hesitation alive in her tone. "What about the driver?" she quickly tacked on.

"No visuals from the marina. Just what we have from your neighbor's doorbell camera. But the police have a BOLO out for the vehicle and a basic description of the driver. I've got Sophie and Robbie making a list of vehicle owners and trying to enhance the doorbell and marina videos the police finally released to us."

"How long will that take?" Ricky asked, worried that they had so little to go on when lives were at stake.

"Robbie says we'll have more from them by midafternoon tomorrow," Trey advised, and in the background he heard Roni call out to his brother.

"I have to go, but I'll keep you posted as soon as we have anything else. In the meantime, sit tight," Trey advised and ended the call.

Ricky stared at the silent phone, frustrated. "Sit tight. I guess he's right. I don't want anyone shooting at us again."

MARIELA FELT THE waves of frustration pouring off Ricky's body. She laid a hand on his forearm as he stood there, still staring at the phone. "They're going to get the information, but…there must be something else we can do."

"I agree. You seemed to know a lot about what was happening at that building site," he said and took hold of her hand.

"You learn a lot when you're taking possible investors around. They would ask questions and I made a point of learning so I could answer," she explained and tugged on his hand. "Go ahead. Ask me."

A small smile inched across his lips. "Why do

you think that they wouldn't be doing more work on that site today?"

With a shrug, she said, "It could be as simple as they're waiting on an inspection or found problems with the foundation."

Ricky wagged his head back and forth, considering what she'd said. "Who would know what's happening?"

"Lots of people," she said with another shrug. "Jorge, of course. The engineers on the project. Inspectors—"

"Think lower down the food chain. People who might be willing to speak to us," Ricky said and, with a tug on her hand, led her to the edge of the mat where they picked up their shoes and walked out into the main living space on the first floor. His parents had gone up to their wing shortly after dinner and the area was empty.

Soft light bathed the space from some table lamps on either side of the room, creating a welcoming feel.

They sat on a sofa that faced windows offering views of the stunning vista beyond. The pool and gardens. The canal, the skyline of Miami and the waters of Biscayne Bay.

Once she'd sat, she said, "Lower in the food chain? The foreman. Assistant foreman. Of course, the workers. They talk a lot about what's happening on the site because their jobs depend on it going well."

Ricky faced her on the couch and took hold of both of her hands. "Is there anyone who would speak to you? Who you trust? Like one of those workers?"

Trust? It had been so long since she'd thought she could trust anyone. She'd been too busy helping Jorge to build any real friendships. When she'd gone to her parents about her divorce, they hadn't understood why she would want to leave Jorge. In their minds he'd given her and them so much. So much that they stood to lose.

"Mariela?" Ricky pressed at her prolonged silence.

"Maybe one of the foremen. Rafael Lopez. We became friendly, especially once I recommended him to become the head foreman when Jorge had to fire the other one," she said, recalling how grateful Rafael had been that she'd spoken up for him.

Ricky nodded. "Do you think he'd talk to you? Tell you what's happening at the site?"

"Maybe," she said, possibly a little too quickly. Rafael had a wife and children. Talking to her might risk his job, but she hoped he was an honest man who would speak out if there was something wrong at the location.

"We can reach out to him. See what he says," she said, didn't wait for him to answer and pulled her cell phone out of her pocket.

"Or we could sit tight," Ricky said, repeating his brother's earlier instructions.

"Is that what you really want to do?" she asked, held up her cell phone and gestured to him with it.

"No. I want to get to the bottom of this. Too much is at stake."

Chapter Twelve

He'd missed them again and cursed himself for how he'd blundered. It had been silly to try and take them out on open water and he'd been careless when driving away from the marina where he'd ditched the stolen Sea-Doo.

The BOLO on the BMW had come across the police scanner, warning him that he had to be more careful. He had to wait for the right opportunity to strike out once more.

Being impatient would not do him any good. It wouldn't help him accomplish his goal.

Patience, he counseled himself, turned up the police scanner to see if they had any more info on him and poured himself a drink.

Taking a sip of the rum, he smiled when nothing else came across the scanner about him and the BMW and planned out his next steps.

RAFAEL LOPEZ HAD been hesitant to speak to her at first. When she'd called, it had almost been impossible to hear him over the excited laughter of his children in the background. She'd worried he'd hang up, until she'd mentioned her fears that someone might get hurt if he didn't help them. At that mention, he'd reluctantly agreed to meet with her the next morning and given her the name of a small café in South Beach.

Ricky and she sat in the café the next morning, waiting for Rafael to show up. She tapped her foot nervously, not sure that he would come as he had promised. Peering around the café, she didn't see any familiar faces or any workmen. The location was in the heart of South Beach on Collins and filled mostly with tourists and beachgoers picking up coffees and breakfast.

They had ordered breakfast also as they waited. *Cafés con leche* and toasted Cuban bread. Across from her Ricky dipped his bread into the coffee and ate, but it was almost mechanical, like something he had to do to keep patient as they waited and waited.

She looked around again, but there was no sign of Rafael. Peering at Ricky's phone, she said, "Any news?" They had given Rafael Ricky's phone number because at Sophie's suggestion earlier that morning, they'd disabled her phone, worried that Jorge had been tracking her.

It made sense because there was no other way anyone could know that they'd gone to Ricky's house and then to the new construction site.

She picked up her piece of toast and nibbled on

it, not really hungry either. Nerves had killed her appetite and, like Ricky, she just needed something to do to keep from going crazy during their wait. She had finished her bread and *café con leche* and almost given up hope when Rafael hurried through the door.

He wore faded jeans and a denim work shirt tossed over a T-shirt. Heavy work boots clomped on the tile floor as he walked over to them.

She stood as he approached and introduced the two men. "Rafael Lopez. Meet Ricky Gonzalez. He and his family—"

"I know who his family is. But why are they involved?" Rafael asked and slipped into a seat across from her at the table.

She worried about telling Rafael too much, but then again, he was risking a great deal to meet them. "Someone attacked me the other night."

"And shot up his house," Rafael jumped in and gestured with a work-roughened hand in Ricky's direction. "It was all over the news."

"It was," Ricky acknowledged with a curt nod. "We think someone did that because Mariela knows something major is wrong with one of Hernandez's latest projects."

"They want to keep her quiet?" Lopez said and pointed to his chest. "I have a family, *mano*. I can't be involved in anything that could hurt them."

"We understand. We won't betray your trust," Mariela said and covered the foreman's hand with her own. It trembled beneath her palm, and he withdrew it quickly, possibly afraid she'd sense his fear.

"And you could be saving lives, Rafael," Ricky urged, clearly trying to appeal to the man's humanity.

Rafael peered down at the tabletop and splayed his thick fingers on the wooden surface. They were workman's hands, nicked and cut in places. Calloused. He ran them back and forth across the surface, and then dipped his head before glancing at them.

"What do you need?"

RICKY HAD DOZENS of questions, but let Mariela take the lead since she understood more about the construction process than he did.

"No one seems to be working on the high-rise condo. Is there something wrong there?" she asked.

Rafael shrugged broad shoulders, stretching tight the fabric of his work shirt with his labor-hard muscles. "The structural engineer inspected and said he wanted the beams deeper, but the pile driver had already been moved to another location. We have to wait for it to come back."

"So nothing's wrong at that location?" Mariela asked.

Rafael dipped his head in confirmation. "*Nada, pero...* The mid-rise passed the inspection the other day, only… I noticed some cracks. That shouldn't be happening. I think they're coming back for more inspections soon."

"You think something was wrong with that first inspection?" Mariela asked while Ricky pulled out his smartphone, tapped in something and then held the phone up for both Rafael and her to see.

"These are the inspection reports. Do the inspectors' names seem familiar?" he asked.

Rafael peered at the names, squinting, and when the foreman sat back, she looked at the reports also, although she had already seen them the other morning.

"I know those two. Smith and Levy. They've inspected a number of our buildings," Rafael said and once again swiped his hands across the surface of the table as if he was clearing away dirt.

"Rafael?" Mariela pressed.

"Sometimes we had a problem and didn't pass. I'd get the men to work on fixing the issues, but sometimes before we did, I'd be told that we were good to go," Rafael admitted.

"Good to go as in you had passed the inspection?" Ricky asked, wanting to make sure he understood what the other man was saying.

"*Sí.* Like we had passed, only I don't remember any new inspections," the other man said and shot to his feet. "I have to go, or I'll be late for work."

He started to walk away, but Mariela stopped

him with a gentle touch on his arm. "Do you remember which properties, Rafael?"

The man nodded. "I'll send you a list. Later. I have to get to work," he said and rushed off.

Ricky stared at his back as the foreman hurried from the café and walked down the block. "He seems like a good man."

"He is," Mariela said and sipped the last little bit of her coffee, which was lukewarm by now.

"Do you think he'll send us a list?" Ricky asked, worried that the other man might reconsider if he thought it might endanger his family to assist them.

Mariela's brow furrowed as she considered his question. But then she nodded and said, "I do. But he said later. What do we do in the meantime?"

As if in answer, his phone pinged. A message from Sophie and Robbie. Here's a list of lawsuits filed against the developer.

He held up the phone for Mariela to see the message. "Looks like we have some homework to do."

THE LIST OF lawsuits was longer than she had expected.

She had occasionally overheard Jorge talking to his attorney about one of the actions, but when she'd asked, he'd always blown her off, telling her it was nothing for her to worry about. Seeing the list made her wonder how Jorge had managed to keep it all from her and what would happen if he lost the lawsuits.

"There are so many," she said as she ran her finger down the list of well over a dozen legal actions against her ex's company.

"There are. Let's find out which properties are involved in the lawsuits and cross-reference that against the inspectors who worked on them," Ricky said as they sat beside each other at the table in his father's study.

Mariela grabbed a pad and pen from the center of the table while Ricky manned the laptop to get the addresses of the buildings involved in the legal actions. "Could you let me have the names of the people suing also? Maybe we can reach out to them for more information," she said.

"Got it." He worked off the list that Sophie and Robbie had produced. One by one he got the information for the addresses and plaintiffs and read them off to her.

It seemed like it took forever to organize the information. They had just finished when Ricky's mother came in together with Josie, who was wheeling a service cart that held several dishes, glasses and an assortment of sodas.

"We thought you might be hungry since it's lunch hour," she said as Josie whipped the tops off the plates to reveal Cuban sandwiches and plantain chips.

"That's so nice of you," Mariela said and rose to hug the other two women.

"Anytime. Besides, Ricky can be a bear if he's hungry," Samantha said with a laugh. "Will you be around for dinner?" she asked with an arch of a brow.

RICKY WAS WELL aware of what his mother was asking with that tone. She probably knew Trey had told them to sit tight and was worried that Ricky wouldn't listen and do something else that was risky. But as much as he always appreciated his mother's concern, he was a grown man who could take care of himself.

"I don't know, *mami*. We may have to step out to speak to some people," he said.

"Ricky—" she began.

But he cut her off with, "We'll be fine."

His mom's lips tightened into a knife-sharp line. "I understand," she said even though it was obvious she didn't.

After his mother and Josie had left, he hopped to his feet to grab them sodas while Mariela placed the plates with the sandwiches on the table. Once they had sat down to eat and continue working, Mariela said, "Your mom is very nice."

Much as he had heard the silent question in his mother's voice, what Mariela hadn't said was as clear to him. "But she worries too much."

"It must be hard to see her family in danger,"

Mariela said and nibbled on one of the halves of the Cuban sandwich.

"It is. It almost broke my heart to hear her crying if my dad was hurt and when Trey was shot several weeks ago," he said and took a bite of his sandwich. The roast pork had the overtones of a citrus marinade, the ham was sweet, the swiss cheese nutty and the final touches of yellow mustard and pickles just helped boost all the different flavors in the sandwich.

"It must be scary," she said and munched on a few of the crispy plantain chips.

"It's not as scary now that they're both with the agency."

Mariela chewed on the chips thoughtfully. "But you're with the agency also, right?"

Ricky did a hesitant shrug. "Yes and no."

Mariela's puzzled look pressed him for more and he said, "I assist them on cases with people who might have issues with trauma or abuse. Sometimes I help profile possible suspects, even though that's not really my thing."

A long pause followed, and Mariela bit her lower lip before she blurted out, "People like me. Clients like me."

Ricky sucked in a deep breath and trapped it before he released it slowly. "I don't think of you as a client. Not anymore," he admitted.

She did a little half smile, and as he met her

gaze, her emerald eyes glittered with joy. "I'm glad you don't."

She was too much to resist. He cupped her cheek and leaned forward until their lips were barely an inch apart. But he hesitated and said, "Are you sure?"

Chapter Thirteen

"I am," Mariela said and closed the distance between them.

His lips were warm, soft at first, but as the kiss intensified, they became harder. More insistent, and something about that, about the force of it, sent a shiver of fear through her.

Sensing it, Ricky tempered his kiss and inched away, but he stroked his thumb across her cheek and then down across her lips. "I would never hurt you, Mariela."

"I know, it's just... I know," she repeated, reminding herself that Ricky was nothing like Jorge. He was thoughtful and caring. The kind of man a woman would want at her side as a partner. But she'd sensed he had his demons as well.

"Let's finish this up and see who the inspectors were," Ricky said and settled back into his chair, giving her needed space.

They went back to work, adding the names of the individuals who had inspected each of the projects to Mariela's list. Time and time again the same names came up.

"It's too much coincidence," Ricky said, leaned back and stroked his chin while reviewing the list.

"What do we do now?" she asked, skimming the names with a finger.

Ricky looked at his watch and then at the list again. "Let's get phone numbers for these plaintiffs and call to see if they'll talk to us. If they won't, maybe their attorneys will."

"I'm Jorge's ex-wife. Do you actually think they'll talk to me?" Mariela said and pushed the pad toward Ricky.

"Good point. But you're not named in any of the lawsuits," Ricky said.

Mariela raked her hair back with her fingers. "Still, his ex. For all they know, I had something to do with whatever shady stuff went on."

Ricky nodded and blew out a rough sigh. "They may not think it was shady stuff, just bad construction."

Mariela hadn't thought there was anything underhanded at first either. By the time she'd had serious misgivings about Jorge's business dealings, she'd been too busy avoiding his barbed words and then his fists. Between that, school and her parents' illnesses, she hadn't been able to do anything but focus on how to get out of her abusive marriage.

"You can't blame yourself," Ricky said, clearly sensitive to what she was thinking.

In truth, she didn't blame herself. "I'm not. I was just trying to survive, but I want to make things right."

Ricky stroked his hand across her back, his touch reassuring. "We will. Together."

"Together," she said, grateful that she no longer had to bear the burden alone.

He held up the pad of paper and smiled. "Let's make those calls."

RICKY STOOD BY Trey as his brother poured Scotch into glasses for the men.

Roni, Mariela and their mom had stepped out for an after-dinner stroll in the garden.

"How's your part of the investigation going?" Trey asked and handed him a glass.

"Good. We've put together a list of problem properties and the building inspectors who worked on them. We have a few meetings lined up for tomorrow to chat with the condo owners and one of the lawyers," he said and walked to the living room sofa.

His father sat in one of the wing chairs across from the sofa and Trey detoured there to hand his father a glass before sitting beside Ricky. But instead of sitting, Trey stood there and sipped his Scotch, his face slightly downturned.

"Spit it out, Trey," Ricky said, well familiar with his brother's avoidance mode.

"The police haven't made a lot of progress on finding the BMW. Sophie, Robbie and me either. But there is some good news. They got some partial prints from Mariela's sliding door and they're running them through the system," Trey said, a glower on his face.

"It is good news. Why the face?" he asked, puzzled by his brother's upset.

Trey shook his head. "It just doesn't feel like enough to keep you safe," he said and took a big slug of his Scotch.

Ricky stared down at his glass and swirled around the ice and liquor. "We were careful to make sure no one was following us. Nothing happened today. Sophie was right that Hernandez must have had a tracker on Mariela's phone."

Trey pointed to him with the hand that held the glass. "I should have thought of that right off the bat."

Maybe he should have, but Trey had had a lot on his mind lately. Before he could point it out, their father did.

"*Mi'jo*, you've had a lot going on. Leaving the force. Your engagement to Roni. And I've put a lot of responsibility on you at the agency. I should have thought about the phone being tracked as well."

"I won't make a mistake like that again, Ricky.

I promise," Trey said and finally plopped onto the sofa next to him.

The slight grate of the sliding French door warned that the women were coming in from their walk.

Mariela and his mother were strolling arm in arm like old friends. Roni had her head tucked close to Mariela's and all the women were smiling, like they didn't have a care in the world. It reminded him of how strong his mother had been no matter what had been going on in their lives. She had always put on a brave face for them. Always made them feel things would be okay no matter how hard it had been at times.

Much like the three women were doing right now.

When they neared, his mother slipped her arm from Mariela, who strolled over and sat to his right. His mother took the wing chair beside his father and Roni slipped in beside Trey on the large leather sofa.

The only thing that kept it from being a homey family scene was Mia's absence, but no sooner had he thought it than Mia came bounding in with Carolina. The Twins waltzed over, kissed everyone in welcome and hauled over two chairs from the nearby dining area table.

"Looks like you're heading to a party," he said, taking in the expensive dresses and heels the two were wearing.

"Going over to the Del Sol," Mia said and a blush worked across her cheeks.

"Going to see John Wilson? The millionaire gamer?" Trey said, and the color deepened even more.

"He's not what he seems, and he's given me some info on Hernandez," Mia said defensively and raised her chin a defiant inch.

"What kind of info?" Ricky asked, wondering what someone like Wilson would be doing with Mariela's husband.

"Apparently Hernandez had heard that Wilson was looking for a location for a new software company he's created. He offered to sell him one of the properties he's just starting to develop. John—"

"It's John now?" Trey teased with the arch of a dark brow.

Mia rolled her eyes and lifted her hand to ask Carolina to finish the story.

"John asked around to other real estate types. We did, too. Wives. Household staff. Rumor is that Hernandez is seriously in debt and may not have enough to complete his high-rise project unless he can offload the mid-rise development," Carolina said.

"We think there's something funky with that project," Ricky explained.

"Why is that, *mi'jo*?" his father asked.

Ricky shared a look with Mariela and, at her nod, he said, "A reliable source."

"How reliable?" Trey pushed.

"We're not at liberty to say," Ricky replied, honoring their promise to Rafael.

Trey waited a beat, but then nodded. "It's late, but I'll call Sophie and Robbie and have them get as much information as they can about that project. Blueprints and things like that."

"We've already reviewed the inspection reports. We have meetings with people suing about other projects to see what they have to say," Ricky advised the larger group, repeating what he'd told Trey and his father earlier.

Mariela jumped in with, "We think there may be problems with other buildings."

"You'll both keep us posted on what you find?" his father said.

"And you'll all be careful," his mother tacked on, ever the Mama Bear.

"We will," Trey and he said in almost unison, drawing chuckles from both parents.

"Well, we'd love to stay, but we've got to make our entrance at the Del Sol," Mia said, shot onto her three-inch heels and smoothed the black fabric of her dress over her generous curves. Carolina also stood and tugged the hem of her silver dress lower over her thighs.

"Say hello to John, for me," Roni said. She had

met the reclusive millionaire while undercover on her last investigation.

"I will. By the way, he says you should come by and game with him again. You're the best so far," Mia said with a smile and wink at Trey, who wrapped a possessive arm around Roni. Payback for his earlier teasing.

"I'll think about it," Roni said with a chuckle.

The Twins waved goodbye and rushed out the door, laughing and teasing each other.

"Are they always that upbeat?" Mariela whispered in his ear.

"Mostly, but they can be serious when they need to," he said, remembering their worry when Trey had been shot just several weeks earlier.

"Time for us to go, too. I'm on the early shift tomorrow," Roni said, rose and extended a hand to her fiancé, coupled with a wink.

Ricky bit back any comment on the wink because he was very happy that Trey finally had more in his life than his old cop job.

The couple gave their goodbyes, leaving Ricky and Mariela alone with his parents. But not for long. Barely a minute had passed when his father stood and gestured for his wife to join him. His mother rose, slipped her hand into his father's and tucked herself into his side, the gesture heartwarming. So loving.

"It's time for us to give you some privacy," his father said.

Privacy? Ricky thought and peeked at Mariela.

Like Mia before her, hot color flooded Mariela's cheeks.

"Thank you, but we were just going to go back to work," he lied, wanting to dissuade his parents from any thoughts they might have about Mariela and him being together.

As much as he wanted it to happen, he didn't want to rush it.

His mother and father shared a look, clearly not believing him. But they didn't press the issue.

"We'll see you in the morning," his mother said and, with a wave, his parents walked up the stairs, hand in hand, heads bent together. At something his father said, his mother chuckled and dropped a kiss on his cheek.

"They're still so in love. Roni and Trey, too," Mariela said with a heartfelt sigh.

"They are. It gives me hope I can have the same thing one day," he said and gazed at her, but she looked away, clearly unsettled by his words.

"Hopefully. I guess we should go up, too, and get some rest. Tomorrow is going to be a busy day." She almost jumped to her feet and nervously slapped her thighs with her hands.

She wasn't wrong about tomorrow. With all the meetings they'd set up for the next day, they'd be very busy.

He stood and walked with her up the stairs, but not side by side, giving her some distance to make her feel more at ease. At her door, she stopped to look at him and it was obvious she needed space that night.

Because of that, he stuffed his hands into his jeans pockets to keep from touching her. "Have a good night."

"Good night and thank you for everything, Ricky." She rocked to-and-fro on her feet for a second before dropping a quick kiss on his cheek and rushing into her room.

He stood there for a long moment, staring at the closed door. But then he turned and hurried down to his father's study.

He was too wound up to sleep and intended to go over all the information they had gleaned that day. Hopefully he would find something else that would tell them what Jorge was doing that was important enough to kill for.

Chapter Fourteen

"I hope you understand why I'm reticent to discuss my client's lawsuit in the presence of Ms. Hernandez," the attorney said and leaned back in his chair. He placed his elbows on the arms, brought his fingers to his lips and stared from Ricky to her over and over.

Mariela leaned forward in her chair and said, "We're divorced, and it wasn't amicable, Mr. Angelo."

The attorney remained silent, glaring at them.

"We won't waste any more of your time," Ricky said and popped out of his chair.

Mariela was about to follow him when the attorney surged forward and opened the file that had been sitting on his desk when they had first walked in.

"Sit down, Mr. Gonzalez," he said and pulled a thick sheaf of papers from the file. He pushed them toward the edge of the desk. "I know your family quite well."

Ricky's lips tightened into a harsh slash. "We'd

like your assistance because it's the right thing to do, not to earn brownie points with my family."

"Call it whatever you like. That's a structural engineer's report on the property. The building was constructed on reclaimed land," the attorney explained.

"But many buildings in Miami and in other coastal cities are built on reclaimed land," Mariela said.

"And most of the Netherlands," the attorney replied and continued. "The issue is that it was improperly constructed. Based on the state of the ground beneath the building, the support beams should have been driven deeper."

Just like the beams on the high-rise structure, Mariela thought.

"Is that what the other homeowners are alleging?" Ricky asked.

Mr. Angelo nodded. "They are. We tried to initiate the lawsuits as a class action, but we didn't have enough people to do that. It's why there are so many legal actions instead of one."

"May we make a copy?" Ricky asked and held up the report.

The attorney waved his hand at it. "That's a copy I made for you."

"We appreciate it," Mariela said and stood, sensing that their time with the attorney was up.

Ricky did the same, but as they headed for the door, the attorney stopped them. "Just another thing. When the condo board first suggested that the residents sue, people were harassed. Little things at first, like flat car tires and elevators that went out of order and took a lot of time to fix."

Mariela didn't miss where he was going. "You said 'at first.'"

The attorney nodded and rose from his chair to join them at the door. "One of the board members got mugged in the parking lot. Another one's car was broken into and trashed. You didn't hear this from me, but a lot of people thought Hernandez was behind it all."

"Thank you for the warning, Mr. Angelo," Ricky said and glanced at her over his shoulder.

"Thanks again for chatting with us," she said and slipped her hand into Ricky's as they left the attorney's office, walked past his assistant and out into the corridor where Ricky stopped to look at her again.

"Maybe we should rethink the visit to the condo owners. We don't want to cause them any more trouble," he said.

"I agree. We can probably get the answers we need over the phone." Answers but not an in-person view of the problems they had sued over.

"Let's head back home and make those calls."

Home. She had to admit his parents' place felt like a home. Maybe because it was filled with family that loved and cared for each other so much.

As they neared Ricky's car, his phone rang, and

he answered. "*Hola, mano*… That's good to hear. We'll meet you there." He paused to look at his watch. "We can be there in about fifteen minutes."

When he finished, he said, "The police have released both our houses. Trey is meeting us at my house so I can see what I need to do to make it habitable. If there's anything you need, we can run by your house afterward."

She held her hands up to shut that down because she still couldn't face going into her home. Being alone again. "I'm good."

He did a little nod. "Let's go. We can phone the condo owners on the way and explain our concerns about meeting with them in person."

After he pulled out of the parking lot, they contacted everyone who had agreed to talk to them and, surprisingly, most were still agreeable to having them come by in person as planned.

"My daddy always told me there's only one way to deal with a bully—you have to stand up to them," the last owner had said before hanging up.

"Are you up for the visit?" Ricky asked and shot her a quick look from the corner of his eye as he drove.

"I'm not going to let him scare me away," she said, determined to be in control of her own life. Determined not to be bullied anymore.

RICKY RISKED ANOTHER look at her and the determination was clear in the set of her face and body.

"I'm proud of you, Mariela," he said, truly admiring her for the strength she had shown in standing up for herself by divorcing Jorge and by continuing to take part in this investigation. Someone else might have hidden out to stay safe instead of trying to get to the truth.

"Thank you," she said, and he could tell that it had been a long time since she'd heard those words from someone.

When he turned onto his street just over ten minutes later, Trey's car was parked to one side of the circular drive. Ricky pulled up opposite him, killed the engine and gripped the steering wheel tightly as he stared at his home.

Plywood covered what had once been big picture windows in his living room and office. Bits of glass from the windows and front door littered the ground and bullet holes marred the normally smooth stucco exterior.

"I'm so sorry," Mariela said and hugged him hard, surprising him with the affection.

"Thank you," he said, returned the embrace and held her for long seconds.

A knock on the driver's side glass jerked them apart and Trey bent to peer through the window.

Heat filled his cheeks, but he ignored his brother's knowing grin and shoved the door open, driving Trey away from the car.

He stepped out and his brother walked beside him to the front door, Mariela trailing slightly behind them. "The detectives locked up," Trey said as they stepped onto the small patio at the entrance. A bullet had hit one of the aqua-colored planters flanking the patio and it had broken in two. Dirt and wilted impatiens littered the ground around it.

Ricky took a deep breath, preparing himself for what he would find inside. He slipped in his key, unlocked the door and walked in.

The bulk of the glass from the windows and doors carpeted the hardwood floors of the foyer, living room and his office. Intermixed with the glass were shards from lamps, picture frames and mementos shattered by the fusillade of gunfire.

His brother clapped his back while Mariela slipped an arm around his waist.

"We will fix this, *mano*," Trey said, grasped his shoulder and squeezed.

A soft sob came from beside him and he looked at Mariela. Tears streamed down her face.

He wrapped her in his arms, kissed the top of her head and murmured, "They're just things. They're not what's important."

That quieted her crying, but only a little. He held her, soothing her by running his hand up and down her back as he once again surveyed the damage to his home.

"*Papi* gave me the name of a contractor and I can call him if you want. Hang out here and get some estimates for you," Trey said, his hands tucked into his pants pockets. He rocked on his heels, clearly also upset by what he was seeing.

"That would be great. Mariela and I were supposed to meet with some people this afternoon," Ricky said and quickly tacked on, "That is if you still feel up to it."

SHE WASN'T UP to it, but she owed him for all that he'd done and for what Jorge or his henchman had done to Ricky's home.

"I'm up to it. I want to find out who did this," she said, waving her arm around at the destruction in the rooms. "I want Jorge to pay for all this."

"Between South Beach Security and the police, we will find out who did this and make them pay," Trey replied.

"Like he did when he beat me bad enough to put me in the hospital?" she shot back, eyebrows raised in challenge.

"My uncle is dealing with that. He's pulled that DA's case files and is reviewing them with the head DA," Trey said.

That caught her off guard because she hadn't thought there was anything they could do about the DA's prosecution decisions.

"I didn't realize… Thank you. Again," she said, feeling as if she would never be able to thank them enough for all that they were doing on her behalf.

"You two should get going," Trey said and tipped his head in a go-ahead gesture.

"Thank you for helping out," Ricky said and hugged Trey. He reached over with a hand, inviting her to join him, and she slipped her hand into his.

They hurried out of the house, and as they did so, Ricky took a long look over his shoulder at his home. His face was stern, lips tight, and a hard glitter darkened his blue eyes.

"We will fix this," she said and gently squeezed his hand.

Is it a we? Ricky wondered, worried that there were so many emotions at play with both of them that anything they might be feeling was not trustworthy.

Ignoring that worry, he helped her into the car, got in and drove to the building that was the subject of the lawsuits. Pulling in front of the condos there was nothing in-your-face obvious to say there were structural issues. But when they walked to the front door, he noticed some hairline cracks at the upper corners of the glass doors, and it took a hard pull to open them.

Inside, they went to the elevator. A big Out of Order sign was taped to the metal door.

"I guess he's still punishing them," Mariela said.

"Seems that way. It's the stairs for us," Ricky said and peered up and down the corridor, searching for the entrance to the stairs. It was at the end of the hall, and they hurried there and up the three stories to the first condo unit on their list of interviews.

To their surprise, there were multiple owners present inside.

"We thought it might be easier for you to meet with us all at once. It'll probably avoid repetition," the one man said. He was an older gentleman, probably in his seventies, and he invited them into his unit with a wave of his hand. Once they had stepped in, he took a spot beside a gray-haired woman who Ricky assumed was his wife.

There were two other couples there as well. He guessed the men sitting together on a white wicker sofa were in their thirties and partners, while the other duo was a fortysomething man and woman. The fortysomethings sat in a pair of wing chairs leaving a white wicker love seat for Mariela and him.

The gentleman who had let them in introduced everyone gathered there. "I'm Russ Smith. This is my wife, Betty," he said and laid a hand on his spouse's shoulder. "Tim and Bob are in unit 400. Elaine and Jerry are above them in unit 500."

"Thank you for the introductions. I'm Ricardo Gonzalez and this is Mariela Hernandez," he said, which caused a ripple of surprise and worry to rush over the owners.

Tim stammered, "H-Hernandez, as in—"

"He's my ex. We divorced a year ago because…

he abused me. Physically and mentally," she said, her voice wavering with upset but the truth of her words resonated with the owners.

Bob reached over and grasped Mariela's hand. "It's okay, Mariela. I was once in a similar relationship until I got out. Now I'm incredibly happy with Tim."

"Thank you," she said, and with that awkwardness done, Ricky and Mariela questioned the owners about the problems they had encountered and what Mariela's ex had done in retribution for the lawsuits.

Ricky listened, mentally taking notes. At one point Russ stood, stalked over to the windows to point out the small cracks near the frames and then to a corner of the room where there was a very visible separation between the walls. "Since we're all in the corner condos, we're seeing the settling of the building more visibly than those in the center," he explained.

"And Hernandez can fix the problem," Tim said with an annoyed huff.

"The structural engineer we hired said it would cost a great deal of money," Elaine said and shook her head in frustration.

"He'd rather bully us into forgetting about it, but we won't," Jerry said and patted his wife's hand in a show of unity.

Ricky wouldn't forget about it either, especially

with other tragic building collapses they could never forget.

"Is the elevator being out of order more bullying?" he asked.

Russ shook his head. "Not this time. Mrs. Wilson from 320 somehow broke the door with her shopping cart."

Ricky did another quick look around the condo, taking in some other cracks here and there. Satisfied they had the information they needed, he glanced at Mariela. "I think we're good. How about you?"

She nodded and faced the owners. "Thanks so much for chatting with us. I'm sorry for everything and hope things will work out for you."

"They will. We have a good lawyer and we're sure they'll get this fixed," Russ said, rose and walked them to the door.

Mariela and Ricky exited into the hallway, down the stairs, and when they reached the main floor, they noticed two men working on the elevator while another man in a suit leaned over them, watching what they were doing.

Mariela stopped short and grabbed his arm to stop him. "It's Jorge."

Sensing their arrival, Mariela's ex stood upright and glanced their way. His body tensed and he reached down and grabbed a large wrench from the one workman's tool bag. He walked toward them slowly, slapping the wrench against his one hand in a menacing gesture.

Ricky stepped slightly in front of Mariela and urged her to move with a tug of his hand.

But Jorge blocked their way down the hall. "Mariela. Who's your little boy toy?"

Mariela's ex was a well-built man with a waist starting to thicken a little. He had at least forty or more pounds and a few inches of height on him and the wrench, but Ricky didn't back down.

"Please step aside," Ricky said, voice steady. His gaze even steadier.

Jorge laughed and leaned forward until he was nose-to-nose with Ricky. "Say pretty please."

"Step aside," Ricky repeated and didn't waver in his stance. As one of the owners had said earlier that morning, you had to stand up to bullies.

Jorge hesitated, his glance skipping to where Mariela stood behind Ricky. But then he slowly stepped to the side to let them pass. Despite that, he continued to tap the wrench threateningly and Ricky was sure to keep Mariela's ex in his line of sight, ready to defend them as necessary.

Outside, Mariela wrapped her arm around his waist and urged him to face her. She cradled his face with her hands and said, "Thank you. I'm not sure I could have handled him alone."

With a grin, he said, "You're stronger than you think."

She offered him a sad smile, rose on tiptoes and

kissed him. With the barest whisper before she retreated, she said, "I could love you."

I could love you, too, he thought, wanting to hold her close and show her just how much he could care for her, but the insistent ring of his phone interrupted the moment.

He jerked the phone from his pocket. It was Trey and he answered.

"What's up?" he asked.

"The police have a match on the fingerprints."

Chapter Fifteen

Since Trey, Sophie and Robbie were at work at the South Beach Security offices in downtown Miami, Ricky and she headed there to hear their report on the identity of the person who had attacked her in her home.

Inside the offices dozens of people were hard at work as Trey came out of his office and walked them to one of the conference rooms. Sophie and Robbie were sitting there with their laptops, but rose to greet them when they came in.

Mariela was struck once more by the similarities in the Gonzalez family members, even with the Whitaker cousin tech gurus. The Gonzalez genes were clearly strong.

Once they were seated, Trey went to the head of the table and motioned for the cousins to begin with the report.

A picture snapped on the screen and Mariela gasped as she stared at the face.

"You know this man?" Ricky asked.

Mariela's heart knocked against her ribs, and

she nodded. "I do. His name is Hector Ramirez. He was Jorge's foreman for a few years."

"We pulled up his history, but it didn't reflect that," Sophie said and engaged a second screen with Ramirez's rap sheet and employment records.

"Maybe he was working off the books," Mariela said in explanation and shook her head. "Jorge promised me he'd stop that when I called him on it."

"But in the meantime, Ramirez was collecting unemployment and public assistance, stealing money from the people who really need it," Ricky said in disgust.

"He was lucky your ex hired him at all. Look at that rap sheet. Shoplifting escalated into breaking and entering. Two assault and battery cases, but he only served time for one of them due to a plea deal," Trey said, walked up to the monitor and pointed out the entries on Ramirez's criminal record.

"Is it possible Jorge found that out about his criminal past and fired him?" Ricky asked.

Mariela shook her head. "Jorge fired him because he came to work drunk on a number of occasions. It caused problems on the work site, so Jorge finally had to let him go."

"Your ex knew Ramirez and he has a violent past. That's a perfect recipe for the assault that happened, but I just need to confirm. I assume

Ramirez was never at your parents' house for any reason," Trey said.

Mariela racked her brain and shook her head. "Never. There was no reason for him to go there."

Trey dipped his head and said, "We can relay that info to the detectives on the case. They already have a BOLO out for Ramirez. Hopefully they'll be able to track him down shortly."

Mariela smiled, feeling relief that they had the identity of her attacker and that he would hopefully be behind bars soon.

"That's good news," she said.

"We have more to share," Robbie said and with several taps on his keys he switched out the images on the screen to bring up photos of two different men.

"Do they look familiar to you?" Trey asked.

"I don't think so," Mariela said.

"When Robbie and I compared all the lists of the inspectors and the inspections, these two names kept popping up—James Smith and Elliot Levy."

Ricky nodded and said, "Those were the same names that popped with us."

"But they weren't names I remembered from Jorge's holiday parties," Mariela added and stared at the screens again, but the men's faces still didn't register. "I've never seen these men," she confirmed once more.

The screens flipped to show salary information

for the two individuals as Sophie said, "Salaries for public employees are accessible online. Smith and Levy are both senior building inspectors earning roughly $110,000 per year."

The images on the screen were replaced with ones of upscale homes in some of Miami's more desirable neighborhoods. "Assuming their wives made similar salaries and if this wasn't a first home purchase, they could easily afford between one and one and a half million."

Ricky gestured to the screen. "Those are not one-million-dollar homes."

"You're right," Robbie said, and numbers popped up over the images. "Here are a real estate site's estimates for these home values. Both are roughly between five and six million. Way out of the league for anyone with those building inspector salaries."

"They're on the take. That's the only explanation," Mariela said.

"Or they inherited money from a dead relative," Trey scoffed.

"Is there any way we can legally get their credit reports for more info?" Ricky asked.

Sophie shook her head. "If a person has a 'permissible purpose' they could, but we don't fall into any of those legal purposes."

"What about the police? Or the DA? Isn't there enough here to do something?" Mariela asked, starting to feel frustrated that her ex-husband and these men had been subverting the system for so long and possibly putting people's lives at risk.

"We've already given what we have to *Tia* Elena. We're preparing everything else we have to give to her and *Tio* Jose. But I think we need more info on these newer projects," Trey said and gestured to his cousins, who put up images of the two condo developments on the screens.

Trey walked to the screens and flipped a hand in their direction. "Whoever tried to hurt you did it because of one of these," he said.

"Probably the mid-rise," Ricky said and pointed to that image.

"Why do you say that?" Trey asked.

Ricky locked his gaze with hers and said, "As I mentioned the other day, we spoke to a reliable source who wishes to remain anonymous. They advised that everything seems aboveboard at the high-rise project."

"But not this mid-rise," Trey said and motioned to that image.

"Not that project," Mariela confirmed and repeated what Rafael had told them. "Our source said he noticed cracks in the building that shouldn't be happening already. He was also supposed to send us a list of other projects where he thought something was off with the inspections."

"But you don't have the list yet?" Trey pushed.

Ricky shrugged and said, "Our source was very

worried about what might happen to his loved ones if Hernandez found out that he'd talked."

Trey nodded and glanced at his cousins. "You've already gotten some info online, but is there any way to get more detailed inspection reports, building plans, things like that?"

"We can check it out and try to have something for you by tomorrow," Sophie advised.

"So close and yet still so far away from stopping Hernandez," Ricky said, his frustration obvious.

"But it's so much more than what we started with," Mariela said, filled with optimism that the nightmare would soon be over.

Ricky offered up a strained smile. "You're right. We have a lot and hopefully it will be enough to let *Tio* Jose take action."

"In the meantime, why don't you go home and let us get to work?" Trey said, his tone conciliatory, hoping to calm his brother's worry.

"Good idea. We'll let you get to work and go home. I'm sure *mami* will be busy making dinner for everyone," Ricky said.

"Have her save some for Roni and me. We'll be over later. How about you two?" Trey asked his cousins.

"We can take a short break," Robbie said, but Mariela could tell that his sister would have preferred to just work through the night.

Ricky must have sensed it as well, since he said,

"You can't be all work all the time, Soph. A break may help you think more clearly."

"Sure," she said, but her tone was unconvincing.

"We'll see you all later," Ricky said, and they hurried out of the SBS offices and down to the parking lot and Ricky's car.

It wasn't long before they were traveling along Brickell Avenue up to Biscayne Boulevard and onto the highway to the causeway and Palm Island.

The tracker I installed on Gonzalez's car is working perfectly, he thought.

He patiently watched the blip on the tablet as it neared where he waited.

In his side view mirror, he caught sight of the Audi as it approached and let another car or two pass before he slipped from his parking spot and discreetly followed.

He had to time the attack perfectly. He'd already checked the traffic situation and luckily it was normal, with no accidents or construction to interfere.

Patience, he told himself as they hit the first part of the causeway heading toward Watson Island. He shifted out of his lane to make his move. Once they were past Jungle Island and the children's museum on the island, he had to act.

Luckily Mr. Ricky Responsible was following the speed limit in the right lane, giving him a perfect target for what he intended.

As the causeway swept down to sea level, he hit the accelerator and surged forward.

MARIELA WAS HAPPILY enjoying the sight of Biscayne Bay glittering in the late-afternoon sun, buoyed by her earlier optimism that they would soon have enough info to arrest Jorge and anyone else involved with his crimes.

A sudden jolt ripped her from that happiness.

Someone had hit them from behind. She turned to look and saw the black BMW with the masked driver. Another jolt on the left rear quarter panel sent the car lurching to the right. Ricky battled to keep the car under control, but the BMW sped forward and with another broadside swipe the nose of the Audi pointed toward the edge of the causeway and the waters of Biscayne Bay.

Mariela screamed, but Ricky somehow managed to right the wheel.

The driver of the BMW slammed his car against them again, trying to drive them into the water.

Ricky fought the wheel, turning into the other car, and it was like two rams charging at each other. Metal grated against metal, crunched and groaned as the drivers battled for control.

And then, suddenly, Ricky stomped on the brake and the BMW shot forward toward Biscayne Bay until the driver righted the wheel and sped off.

COLD SWEAT BATHED Ricky's body and every inch of him shook as adrenaline raced across his nerve endings. He brought the car to a halt just feet away from the water.

Somehow instinct took over and he flipped on the hazard lights as he asked, "Are you okay?"

Mariela did a shaky nod. "I'm okay."

"I have to call 911," he said and was about to dial when two police cars pulled up. One slipped behind them while the other took a spot in front of his car.

As an officer stepped up to the window, hand on the gun in his holster, Ricky kept his hands on the wheel until the officer was beside them and bending over to look into the car.

"Ricky? Is that you, *mano*?" the officer asked and leaned an arm on the roof of the car.

Ricky took a longer look at the cop and smiled as he recognized one of Trey's high school friends. "Danny? You're looking good," he managed to say as the earlier fear dissipated.

Danny eyeballed the car. "Sorry you can't say the same. What happened?"

"Someone tried to run us off the road. Black

BMW. Driver was masked," Ricky said and looked at Mariela for confirmation.

"That's what I saw," she said with a nod.

"The BOLO we have in place?" Danny asked and Ricky bobbed his head.

"Probably one and the same," he confirmed.

Danny held up a finger in a "wait" gesture and walked toward the vehicle in front of them, radioing someone as he went. When he reached that vehicle, he and the other officer stood there, listening to what he assumed were instructions.

"What's happening?" Mariela asked, leaning forward to get a better look at the officers.

"They're probably going to have to take the car in as evidence," Ricky said, recalling Trey's many tales over the years of what had happened on his assorted cases.

Sure enough, when Danny returned, he said, "Sorry to do this to you, but we have to secure this scene until the CSI team can process it. If you don't mind stepping from the car, I have a few more questions for you before we let you go."

Ricky gestured to the car and said, "And how will we go, Danny?"

"Trey is on his way, but I'm sure he'll want to stay and make sure we're doing everything by the book," Danny advised with a roll of his eyes and gestured to the other vehicle. "As soon as we're done, I can have Officer Duran take you home. It's not that far to your parents'."

"Thanks." Danny skewered him with cop's eyes, all earlier traces of friendliness gone.

He answered Danny's questions, trying to recall what he could from the moment of the first impact to that second when he'd thought they'd go flying into the waters of Biscayne Bay. It was only something instinctual that had made him stomp on the brake to stop the attack.

"Is that what you remember?" Danny asked Mariela.

She glanced at the car and then back up the road. Jabbing with her finger, she said, "He first hit us as we got near the end of Watson Island."

"And toward the flat part of the causeway?" Danny asked with a raised eyebrow.

She nodded. "It was hit after hit after that. Just like Ricky told you."

Danny jotted some notes down in his pad, slipped the pen into the holder and closed it. "I think I've got what I need for now."

A honk drew their attention and Ricky watched as Trey drove by in his vintage Camaro and parked beyond the police cruiser in front of them. A second later, the CSI unit pulled up behind Danny's cruiser.

"Cavalry has arrived," Danny said and walked away to coordinate with the CSI officers and Trey.

Ricky cupped her cheek and stroked a thumb across the pale color there. "Are you really okay?"

She reached up to take his hand with hers. "I

am. I just don't understand how Jorge's old foreman found us."

"I don't either, but I'm sure Trey and the cops
will find out how," Ricky said as he watched his
brother work with his old colleagues before he
walked over to them.

"Let me take you home," Trey said when he
joined them.

"Will everything be okay?" Ricky asked and
shot his chin up toward the officers and CSI on
the scene.

"They sent their best when they saw your name.
I have no doubt they'll do a thorough investigation," he said and added, "Let's go. I'm sure the
adrenaline is racing through you now, but when
you crash…it'll be better to be home."

Chapter Sixteen

Trey hadn't been wrong, Mariela thought. It had been good to be home because her knees had given out just after they'd reached the house. Samantha had pressed a Scotch into her hand and urged her to sit.

She'd fallen onto the sofa, the ice rattling in the glass until she braced her wobbly hand on the padded arm. Taking a little sip, she let the warmth of it travel down her throat.

Ricky sat beside her, wrapped an arm around her shoulders and drew her close. The heat of his body chased away the last remnants of the chill in her core.

"I don't get how they knew where we were, Trey. We shut down Mariela's phone days ago," Ricky said.

"I know, *mano*. They could have been watching you. It's possible they slipped a tracker on your car as well," Trey said and took a long drag on his Scotch. "CSI should be finished with their initial review of the car. If there's a tracker, we should know soon."

"In the meantime, let's sit down for some supper. Josie and I spent the better part of the day making *ropa vieja* for you," Samantha said, rose and smoothed the fabric of the linen tunic blouse she wore. The telltale gesture gave away how nervous she was despite her outwardly calm actions.

"I love *ropa vieja*. My *mami* and I always made it for my father's birthday," Mariela said, popped to her feet and walked to Samantha's side.

Ricky's mother slipped an arm through hers and they strolled to the dining area of the open concept space, but as Samantha went to go into the kitchen, Mariela said, "Let me help."

"With pleasure," Samantha said, smiling.

RICKY WATCHED HIS mother and Mariela walk away and his heart did a little clench at just how natural it seemed when nothing around him was close to natural.

Someone had just tried to kill them. Again.

And despite all the progress they'd made on what Hernandez was doing, they still didn't have enough to shut down the threat to Mariela and him.

"*Vamos, mi' jo.* You've got to let go of it, if only for a little while," his father said.

"Is that what you did, *papi*? Let go of it?" he asked even though he already knew the answer.

When he thought back to his childhood, it had been about as normal as it could be while his father had been a marine and then a police officer. Of course, the demands of those jobs had been buffeted by the support of his grandparents and the growing success of South Beach Security, especially after his father had left the police force to join his grandfather at the agency. They'd had more stability then, both in terms of a home life and financially.

"It's what you do for your family and for yourself," his father said and urged him to go with him to the dining table across the way.

As he sat, he could hear the gentle murmur of voices from inside the kitchen as Mariela, Josie and his mom worked to prepare dinner. It was a comforting sound, making everything seem almost normal. It made him imagine the moment when every day would be like this and restored some calm to his soul.

Short moments later the women came into the room with plates piled with mounds of rice covered with the shredded beef in tomato sauce. *Ropa vieja* was one of his favorites and his stomach rumbled at the thought of eating.

Mariela placed a plate in front of him. "Thank you," he said.

"You're welcome," she said and walked back to the kitchen. Seconds later she returned with plates with ripe plantains and placed one at either end of the table. When she was done, she sat beside him and Trey, and once his mother took a spot beside his father, they ate.

The meal passed companionably with everyone eating and chatting. Time passed quickly but as the meal was ending, his brother pulled out his cell phone and took a look. His face went from easygoing to all hard sharp lines at whatever he read.

Ricky's earlier calm fled, replaced by worry as he waited to hear what his brother had to say.

"Ricky? Something wrong?" Mariela said from beside him.

"Nothing, *mi amor*," he said, the endearment slipping from his lips unintentionally.

She jumped, startled by it, but then nodded and smiled. "Whatever it is, *mi amor*, we will handle it together," she said, reached beneath the table and took hold of his hand.

Once they were finished, his mother and Mariela rose to clear off the table and Josie came in to help. He noticed that his brother leaned over to say something to his father, who looked his way and jerked his head in the direction of the living room area.

He rose, walked over with them, and they sat on the sofa. Trey took out his phone and flipped to an image. "My CSI contact sent me this," he said.

Ricky peered at the image, puzzled. "Is that a tracker?"

Trey nodded. "It is. Someone planted it beneath the wheel well of your car."

"Any idea when?" his father asked.

Trey shrugged. "The techs are going to try and access its logs. Maybe we'll know then."

"Did Hernandez do this?" Ricky asked.

"Either Hernandez or whoever he hired," Trey suggested. He peered at him, ran a hand through his hair in frustration and said, "I don't like this, Ricky. My gut tells me something else is going on here. Maybe even something that has nothing to do with Mariela."

"Like what?" Ricky asked.

"Something more personal," Trey said and his gaze bounced between them. "What if this is about Ricky? Or the family?"

"That makes no sense, Trey. What would anyone have against me or the family? We help people," Ricky said, unable to believe that it would be some kind of vendetta against the Gonzalez clan.

"We do, but for everyone we help there may be someone who hates us for what we do," his father said and sat back heavily against the sofa cushions.

Ricky's mind whirled with the possibility that maybe he was the one who had brought danger to Mariela.

"I need some air," he said and jumped to his feet.

Mariela had entered the living room with his mother, and he held out a hand to her. "Want to go for a walk?"

RICKY'S DISTRESS WAS there for her to see in the hard lines of his face. In the tension in his body and his hand as she held it. She squeezed it gently, trying to offer comfort as they hurried to the French doors and out onto the grounds.

They strolled around the pool and to the water's edge in silence. They stopped on the dock where Ricky leaned on one of the posts and drew her close to lean against him.

"What's wrong? Did something else happen?" she asked, worried at about how upset he was— almost lost, it seemed to her.

He avoided her gaze and said, "There was a tracker on the car. Trey isn't sure that Jorge is the one responsible for the attack."

She turned in his arms to face him. "That can't be. Who else would do it?" she said and stroked a hand across his chest to soothe him.

"That's what I said," Ricky said with a shake of his head.

"This all started with me visiting your aunt. With someone attacking me," she said and tapped her chest in emphasis.

Ricky looked away and in a soft voice he said, "*Sí*, it did and yet… The shootings and this latest attack. It has to be something really, really big for your ex or his foreman to try that."

Mariela recalled what she had overheard in Jorge's office, and she had no doubt that it was something big. "I think it is, Ricky. Jorge sounded almost frantic that night. I think he would do anything to protect what he's doing. Especially if it could cost him millions."

Ricky nailed her with his gaze. "Let's hope you're right and we can end this danger."

"We will," she said and rose on tiptoes to kiss him. To offer him the same support he had given her.

He returned the kiss, tenderly at first, but as desire grew, he drew her tighter, their bodies pressed together.

Against her belly he hardened, and she shifted against him, needing him in a way she had never thought would be possible again.

"Mariela," he said and encircled her waist in his hands to urge her to stop.

"I want this, Ricky. What I feel with you... It's not anything I ever felt before," she said and cupped his face in her hands, reassuring him that she knew what she wanted.

"It's the same for me, *mi amor*." With a tender smile, he said, "Maybe it's time we go back in."

She grinned. "I'd like that."

They held hands and strolled toward the house, but as they neared, she realized Trey was standing on the back patio, hands on his hips. His face had that stony hard look that she already recognized meant trouble.

That Ricky understood it as well was evident from the way his hand tightened on hers.

They stopped before him and he glanced between them, uneasy.

"Just spit it out," Ricky said, tugged her closer and wrapped an arm around her shoulders to hold her close, as if preparing for a blow.

"The police found Hector Ramirez," Trey said.

Chapter Seventeen

"Where?" Mariela asked and braced for his reply.

"He washed up by the Collins Bridge near Haulover Park," Trey said.

Ricky immediately put two and two together. "Which is right near Hernandez's high-rise condo."

Trey's lips twisted with chagrin. "*Sí*, it is, and I know where you're going with this. There's one big problem. It appears Ramirez was murdered sometime last night."

"That doesn't mean that Hernandez wasn't behind the wheel this afternoon," Ricky pushed because he couldn't get on board with Trey's theory that it might not have to do with Mariela.

Reluctantly, Trey nodded. "You're right. Just call it my cop's instinct that I feel this isn't as cut and dry as you think."

"Are the police going to call Jorge in for questioning about his old foreman?" Mariela asked.

"My contact says that once the ME is finished with the autopsy and they know more, they'll call me and let me know what's up," Trey said and looked back toward the house when someone called his name.

Roni strolled through the house and up to Trey. She kissed him and hugged him hard before greeting them. "How are you handling the news?" she asked.

Ricky shot a quick glance at Mariela, who said, "We're dealing with it."

Roni blew out a harsh breath. "I know how frustrating it can be. Believe me, it's how I feel when I can't get a handle on a case, even when it involved Trey and me."

"I am frustrated, but I know you're all doing your best," Ricky said in resignation.

"We are. Trey and I will keep pressuring the detectives on the case and let you know once we have more," Roni promised and shot a look up at Trey, who nodded to confirm it.

"And Sophie and Robbie will have more info for us in the morning that we'll work on as well," Trey reminded.

"Seems like there's nothing else for us to do tonight," Mariela said.

Roni nodded. "You should get some rest. It could take up to four hours for the ME to finish the autopsy on Ramirez, but we may not have preliminary results for possibly twenty-four hours."

"Like Roni said, we'll keep you posted if anything does happen," Trey added, clearly sensing that Ricky had had enough of the discussion.

"Thanks. You two get some rest as well," Ricky said and leaned in to hug his future sister-in-law and his brother.

Mariela followed his lead to embrace Roni and Trey before taking hold of his hand and walking with him into the house and up the stairs.

In the foyer tucked between the two bedrooms in the wing, he faced her, unsure of whether she'd want to spend some more time with him.

He inched his head in the direction of his room. "Do you feel like having a drink?"

IT SURPRISED HER yet again that she wanted more than just a drink with him, but for now, she'd take that and his company, which she enjoyed immensely.

She wanted to understand him better. What made him tick.

"I'd like that," she said and, at his playful tug, followed him into the room.

There was a large king-size bed as they entered and, at the far end, a small sitting area in the corner, which had a view of the backyard and the waters beyond that.

She sat on the love seat and the cushions enveloped her in their comfiness.

Ricky walked over to a dry bar at one side of

the sitting area, poured them a Scotch and joined her on the love seat.

They sat there in comfortable silence, sipping their drinks, and savoring the sight of downtown Miami and Biscayne Bay. But as she recalled that they had almost ended up in those beautiful waters, she shivered and gulped down a healthy portion of the drink.

Wanting to drive those thoughts from her mind, she said, "How did you decide to become a psychologist?"

Ricky did a little noncommittal shrug. "I'm not really sure, to be honest. I was a book nerd but social also. People just seemed to like telling me their problems and I was good at listening."

"Like you do with the support group," she said, recalling her visit to his office.

"Like that and in the therapy sessions," he admitted and slipped his arm across her shoulders.

"But you work with your family's agency, too," she said, recalling what he'd said before.

"I do. But like my cousin Pepe, I didn't want to be involved. I couldn't see how I could help, but little by little I got drawn in and, truth be told, I don't hate working with my family at SBS," he confessed.

"Your family seems very nice," she said because in all the time that she'd been in contact with them they'd treated her well.

"They're the best even if a little too overprotective at times. Especially my mom, even with everyone at the office. She is our Mama Bear," he said with a laugh.

"Must be nice," Mariela said with a forced smile, but Ricky immediately saw past that to the sadness in her tone.

"It's been a while since someone was nice to you," he said, but it was a statement, not a question.

She mimicked his earlier shrug, slightly uneasy about sharing. With a shaky breath, she said, "It's been a few hard years since my *mami* and *papi* got sick."

"What's wrong with them?" he asked and stroked his hand back and forth her upper arm in a calming gesture.

"*Papi* has the beginning stages of dementia. He could probably still live at home, but *mami* broke her hip and still can't move around all that well."

"You've been taking care of them by yourself? No siblings?" he asked.

"I'm an only child so it's been up to me to pay for the assisted living and keep their house up, hoping that maybe one day they can come home and be with me. That it could be a little bit more like it was when I was younger and they were so full of life and we were happy," she said, trying to hold on to those joyful memories rather than the pain of the present.

"I hope that can happen," he said and sipped

the last of his Scotch. He set the glass on the coffee table in front of him and shifted in the seat slightly to see her better.

"I hope I can, too," she said with a determined dip of her head, trying to convince herself that she'd be able to make that wish come true.

He tucked his hand beneath her chin, applied gentle pressure to urge her to face him and tenderly stroked his thumb across her cheek.

"YOU'RE A GOOD DAUGHTER. A good person," Ricky said, sensing that she had some doubt about her dream of bringing her family back together again.

Her lips twisted up in a half smile and she did a little laugh. "Jorge didn't think so."

"Jorge is an ass," he said and brushed a whisper-soft kiss across her cheek and then down to lightly trace the edges of her lips.

It was a kiss of promise, of invite. He wanted her to accept him and what might be possible between them.

She leaned into him, opening herself to him. Her lips on his, tentative at first, but growing more mobile, more intense, as they kept on kissing until he needed her closer. Needed to feel her, her heartbeat against his, racing as his was.

He leaned back onto the arm of the sofa, urged her to come with him, and she crawled into his lap, her center over him. Over the growing hardness at the feel of her against him.

Breaking apart from her only long enough to say her name, almost as a prayer, he cradled her back in his hands as they kissed over and over.

He opened his mouth and accepted the slide of her tongue, tasting her, a mix of the Scotch and sweetness. *Mariela's sweetness*, he thought with a groan as she shook in his arms.

He didn't want to misread the signals so he shifted away the slightest bit, and husked, "We can stop whenever you want."

"I don't want to stop," she said and stroked her hand across his cheek before tunneling her fingers into his hair and urging him into the kiss again.

IT HAD BEEN too long, maybe never, since she had been treasured this way. As if she was someone special. Someone who deserved to be loved. Someone who could love someone else, love Ricky, with all her heart.

She drifted against him, against the hard planes of his body, relishing the feel of him. The gentle way he clasped her to him, his hands splayed across her back. His body beneath her, between her legs as she straddled him. Hard and growing harder until she had to move on him. Had to have his hands on her.

"Touch me, Ricky. Please, touch me," she said, unafraid because she knew Ricky would never hurt her.

He groaned and his body shook beneath hers,

but he did as she asked, slipping his hand around to cup her breast. Rub his thumb across her hard nipple before tweaking it between his thumb and forefinger.

The action dragged a rough moan from her, and damp flooded her center. When he tempered his touch, she whispered against his lips, "Don't stop. It feels so good."

A harsh breath escaped him along with a needy moan. "You feel so good," he said and brought his other hand around to caress her other breast.

She watched, loving the sight of his hands on her. He had an artist's hands, long and elegant. Strong and yet amazingly tender. Her heart tightened in her chest, and she sucked in a ragged breath. When he bent his head and teethed one hard nipple, she jumped, and her insides clenched with need. The need for him not to stop. The need to feel his mouth on her skin. His hardness buried deep inside her.

Reaching down, she grabbed the hem of the loose blouse she wore and ripped it up and over her head, and as she did so, he reached around and undid the clasp of her bra. Her breasts spilled free, and he immediately kissed her breasts, shifting from one to the other as he loved her with his mouth.

"*Dios*, you are so beautiful," he whispered against her breasts.

His mouth was so warm, so moist, against her.

She clasped his head to her, loving his touch. His care and patience that was driving her to move on him, passion building. Her body tightening as she climbed ever higher.

His hands came down to still her hips and he whispered, "I don't know if I can hold back anymore."

"I don't want you to hold back."

"Dios," RICKY MUTTERED, his body shaking from the desire rushing through him.

Somehow, he didn't know how, he was on his feet with her in his arms, hurrying to the bed on the other side of the room. He let her slip down his body until she was on her feet, slightly wobbly. Laying his hands on her waist, he steadied her while she undid the buttons on his *guayabera* shirt and bared him to her gaze.

Barely a second passed before her hands were on him, smoothing across the muscles of his chest. She shifted them down, the backs of *her* hands skimming his defined abs and lower to cover his erection. Stroke him over the fabric of his jeans, her touch tentative. Hesitant, but he tempered his need, aware of what a big decision this was for her. What a major step considering the nightmare she had suffered during her marriage.

He let her take her time exploring him and she moved her hands all across his body, learning the shape of him, but when she reached for the button on his jeans, he stilled the motion of her hands.

"Let me," he said and instead undid the button and zipper on her jeans and helped her step out of them, leaving her in nothing but a tiny scrap of black cotton around her lush hips.

"So, so beautiful," he said again.

She smiled, a sexy little grin, ran her hands across his chest and said, "So are you."

That smile undid what was left of his restraint. He toed off his shoes and socks, and yanked off his jeans and briefs, hopping from foot to foot in his haste to be with her.

He urged her down onto the bed, shifting with her until they were in the center of the large mattress, side by side. He still wanted to give her space because of her past.

They lay there, touching. Exploring and kissing. Breaths growing ever more hurried as desire climbed ever higher until she slipped her hands to his shoulders and urged him over her, inviting him to join with her.

"Just a second," he said. He rushed off the bed and searched his pants for his wallet. When he found it, he pulled out a condom and hoped that it hadn't expired.

As he climbed back toward her, she reached out and took the condom from his hand, tore the foil wrapper and removed it with shaky hands.

He held his hand out for it, but she shook her head. "No. I want to do it."

He nodded, understanding her need to be in control. To be the one to decide how and when. He was the lucky man who had earned her trust and he didn't intend to shatter that trust.

He sat back against the pillows and headboard, and she straddled him, slowly unrolled the condom down his length. It was all he could do not to lose it and he gritted his teeth to hold on until she rose above him.

With hands slightly unsteady from the force of his passion, he guided her down and she took him in, the heat and tightness of her surrounding him.

"Ricky," she said, voice husky, her emerald gaze almost black with desire.

"Whatever you want, *mi amor.* I'm here for you," he said and swept his hand up to tenderly cup her jaw.

She worried her lower lip and shot a quick glance down at her breasts, silently communicating her request.

He leaned forward and kissed the hard tip, lightly teethed it while caressing her other breast with his fingers.

She moaned, held his head to her and moved, shifting her hips on him. Heightening passion that was already seriously on the edge.

When he sucked her nipple a touch harder, tweaked the other tight tip with his fingers, a rough gasp escaped her and she ground down on him, seeking her release.

"Let go, *mi amor*. I'm here to catch you when you fall," he said and splayed his hands across her back.

She bent and tucked her head against his, her breath ragged, almost wild, as she rode him.

His own breath grew more erratic as he battled to maintain control, wanting her to have her release before he lost it.

"Ricky, please," she pleaded and held on to his shoulders as she rolled onto her back and took him with her. "Please," she said again, her gaze locked on his.

He let go of his tenuous grasp and drove into her, his thrusts coming harder and faster as her soft cries urged him on. Inside him the pressure built until he couldn't hold back any longer.

With one last powerful thrust, he came, but as he did so she arched upward and dug her fingers into his back, calling his name.

His arms shook as he held his weight off her body until she stroked her hands up his arms and urged him down onto her.

"I'm too heavy," he said, and in response, she tightened her arms around him.

"You're just right," she said, a satisfied smile on her face. She stroked her hands up and down his back, and he let himself enjoy the aftermath of their lovemaking.

As her breathing slowed, he finally slipped to her side. "I'll be back," he said, needing to clean up.

"I'm not going anywhere," she teased, her tone lighthearted and a smile on her face that made her remarkable emerald eyes glitter brightly.

He took her words to heart, knowing just how much courage it had taken for her to trust him with her body and hopefully with her heart.

Rushing to the bathroom, he quickly washed up and returned to bed. She was already fast asleep, one hand tucked under cheek, her other hand resting on his spot in the bed, as if reaching out for him.

He slipped into bed and beneath her arm. At the contact, she stirred and shifted toward him, pressing her body to his, a smile still on her face.

Grinning, he wrapped an arm around her waist, and closed his eyes, but his mind whirled with all that had happened that day and thoughts of what they might encounter in the days to come.

No matter how hard it might be, he hoped they would continue on the journey they had just begun that night.

Chapter Eighteen

The thoughts that had chased Ricky to sleep jerked him from the bed early the next morning.

He tucked the covers in around Mariela and tossed on some clothes to go get himself a cup of coffee before calling Trey to see if he had any news on the Ramirez homicide or from Sophie and Robbie.

To his surprise, Trey was sitting at the dining area table with their father, having coffee and a huge mound of eggs, bacon and Cuban toast. His brother had just forked up a large portion of eggs when he spotted Ricky.

With a knowing grin, Trey said, "You look like you had a good night."

"Don't you have a home?" Ricky teased back and went to a serving cart to make himself a *café con leche* with the carafe of Cuban coffee and scalded milk on the cart.

After Trey swallowed, he grinned and said, "I do, but Roni had to go in early and Josie knows what I like for breakfast."

"It was meant to be rhetorical, *mano*," he said, not ready to deal with any comments from either Trey or his father, who had arched a brow at Trey's earlier comment and was clearly wondering what was going on between his two sons.

"Is everything…okay with Mariela?" his father asked, raising one thick salt-and-pepper brow in question.

"Everything is more than okay, *papi*. The only thing that would make it better would be for us to finish this investigation so Mariela can get on with her life," he said, took a sip of his coffee and added more sugar to his cup.

"And you with yours?" his father said, worry and disapproval twined together in his tone.

"Mariela is a good woman," he shot back, and his brother held up one hand in a stop gesture.

"No one is implying she isn't. It's just a little bit sudden," Trey said and set his fork down, his appetite apparently gone.

"Like you and Roni aren't?" he challenged, but guilt immediately swamped him with the realization that they were just worrying about him the way he'd worried about Trey.

"I'm sorry. I get it. Family worries about family," he said and sat down in between his brother and his father, who was at the head of the table.

Silence reigned for a moment until Trey picked up his fork and said, "The detectives on the Ramirez case have preliminary info from the

ME. Time of death for Ramirez is around midnight the night before."

"Which confirms he couldn't have been the person driving the BMW that attacked us yesterday," Ricky said.

"It does, *mi'jo*," his father said with a nod and continued. "Hernandez must have had a falling-out with his old foreman and killed him. It's possible he either did the attack himself or found someone else to help him."

Trey made a face, prompting Ricky to ask, "But you think otherwise."

"Possibly. Like I said yesterday, something is rubbing me the wrong way about the last three attacks," Trey said and picked up his cup of coffee.

Trey had been an excellent cop with great instincts about the cases he worked on, but Ricky couldn't understand why his brother seemed so hesitant about this one.

"If it isn't Hernandez behind these attacks, who is it?" he asked.

Trey's lips thinned into a harsh line. "I don't know, but we will find out. The detectives are sending over the preliminary report shortly. As soon as we have it, we can review it and decide what our next steps should be."

SUNLIGHT FILTERED BETWEEN her semiclosed lashes, and Mariela screwed them shut. She didn't want to get out of bed. She just wanted to lay there with

Ricky and enjoy the morning, but as she reached out, she realized he was already gone.

She stretched to work out a morning kink and as she did so the slight soreness between her legs reminded her of what they had done last night. How they'd made love and then woken again in the middle of the night to pleasure each other when Ricky hadn't been able to locate another condom.

Her insides clenched with the memory of how he'd satisfied her over and over again and how she'd made him quake and shout her name.

She'd never expected to be intimate with a man again quite so soon. Then again, Ricky wasn't just any man.

And despite last night's very satisfying love-making, if they were to consider anything remotely permanent in a relationship, they had to get rid of the specter of Jorge and the danger he brought to them first.

Filled with that concern, she hurried from bed to take a shower and prepare for what she guessed would be another challenging day. Hopefully the police and Ricky's cousins would have information that moved along the investigation.

Although she wanted to luxuriate beneath the spray of hot water and memories of the night before, she rushed through the shower, got dressed and went into the bedroom she'd been using to make it seem as if she'd slept there. The last thing she needed was household gossip about her and Ricky.

She was about to head down when she ran into Samantha at the top of the stairs. As the older woman narrowed her gaze to peer at her, a rush of heat swept up from Mariela's neck to her face at the thought that Ricky's mom might have guessed what had happened with her son last night.

"How are you feeling? You look a little flushed," Samantha said as they walked down the wide flight of stairs to the ground floor.

"My room was a little warm," she lied.

"I'll have someone check the thermostat," Samantha said, but Mariela waved her hands.

"No, it's okay. I was actually quite comfortable," she said.

Samantha glanced toward the dining area table where Ricky had turned and was watching Mariela intently. With a wry grin, Samantha said, "I'm sure you were."

Mariela muttered a silent curse and bit her lip, sure that his mother was aware of what had gone on last night.

As they neared the table, the men rose and gestured for them to sit. Ricky's father kissed his wife on the cheek and said, "We were just going into my study to review the ME report Trey received."

"I guess Mariela and I will take our coffee there," Samantha said.

"No need, *mi amor*. We can handle this," Ramon said, but his wife held up a hand to stop him.

"If it involves my family's safety, I intend to be a part of it and I'm sure Mariela wants to know what's planned as well," Samantha said, steel in her voice. Then she turned to Mariela and said, "How do you like your coffee and would you like anything else for breakfast?"

"Just coffee, thanks. Light and sweet," she said and walked over to take the coffee and wait for Samantha as she prepared her own mug.

When his mother finished, she said, "We're ready now."

Ramon did a little bow and, with a flourish, waved his hand in the direction of his study. "After you, *mi amor*."

"Thank you," Samantha said, and together they walked into her husband's study and took seats at the table.

The three men joined them just seconds later, but as Trey grabbed a laptop, he glanced at them and said, "The photos may be graphic."

"Are you okay with that, Mariela?" Ricky asked, concern evident in his voice.

"I can handle it." After all, she'd seen Jorge's violence firsthand.

With a nod, Trey popped the report onto the large monitor on the one wall of the office and recited pertinent facts from it while they followed along. "As I told Ricky and *papi* earlier, time of death was around midnight the night before, which rules him out of the road attack. Cause of death was strangulation using a thin nylon rope."

Trey shifted from the written report to a photo of a length of bright purple nylon rope and her stomach roiled at the sight of it. A chill sweat washed over her body and Ricky's arm was immediately around her shoulders.

"What's wrong?" he asked, seeing her upset response to the photo.

Memories pummeled her but somehow she wrestled them back, and with a shaky breath, she said, "Jorge had rope just like that. He used it to tie me up and rape me."

"Mariela, *Dios*," Ricky said and waved at Trey to flip away from the photo.

His brother did as he was asked and in a sympathetic voice said, "Are you sure?"

Mariela was looking away at first, but then she slowly, almost regally, lifted her face and said, "I'm sure. He used to keep the rope in the garage to tie down things if a storm was coming."

To tie down things he didn't want to lose, Mariela being just another of his things, Ricky thought. Rage filled him at what she'd suffered, but he had to keep a level head for all their sakes.

"Will that info help in getting a search warrant?" he asked.

Trey shrugged. "Possibly. I can pass that info

on to the detectives handling the case. If Hernandez consents to them looking around, he might be cocky enough not to have hidden it."

"You said Ramirez washed up around the Collins Bridge and Haulover Park. Any chance of any CCTVs in the area catching something?" Ricky asked.

"Detectives are already trying to get that info," Trey advised.

His father drummed his fingers on the tabletop and said, "Does your ex have a security system with cameras?"

Mariela nodded. "He does. Both at the house and the office. The Equinox Security Group installed it and monitors it."

"Equinox. That's our provider as well, isn't it?" his father said.

"It is. I'll see if they can do us a favor. Sophie and Robbie can also get to work on checking webcams in the area," Trey said, snatched the speakerphone from the tabletop and called their cousins.

"Good morning. How's the info on those inspectors going?" Trey asked.

"Just finishing up but I can tell you that almost every time one of Hernandez's buildings had a failed inspection, either Smith or Levy would show up and make it right somehow," Sophie said.

Robbie chimed in with, "Not that there's anything minor when you're talking about construction projects, but some were for minor electrical issues. Others were for plumbing. The ones that really stick out are when foundation issues were suddenly cleared."

Ricky shared a look with Mariela and said, "We have a source who says he noticed unusual cracks and issues on Hernandez's new mid-rise project."

"Smith worked on that one and approved it, but for some reason another inspection was requested. The second inspection has been outstanding for some time," Sophie said.

"And if Levy gets it, he'll just approve it," Mariela said with an exasperated sigh.

"He probably will," Robbie agreed.

"If that foundation is compromised, couldn't the whole structure collapse?" Samantha asked.

"It could if it's very compromised. There's no way to know for sure how bad it is without an independent inspection of the foundation and the ground beneath it," Sophie advised.

"Is that because the project is on reclaimed land?" Ricky asked, recalling the discussion they'd had about the issues with the one condo where they'd visited with the owners.

"It is. If the land beneath isn't properly compacted, it could cause all kinds of problems including the influx of water that would weaken the area even more," Sophie said.

"Thanks, Sophie. We need your help with something else," Trey said and provided their cousins with the information about the areas and times where they needed them to check for web-cam footage.

"I'll get on it right away while Sophie finishes up the report on the inspectors," Robbie said and ended the call.

"We need to take a look at that mid-rise location," Ricky said and peered around the table at everyone gathered there.

"Didn't Mia mention that Hernandez was trying to offload one of those properties to John Wilson?" his mother said.

"She did," Ricky confirmed.

"Maybe Wilson can help us out and take a look," Mariela suggested, and everyone around the table nodded.

"It looks like we have our work cut out for us. I'll coordinate with the detectives on all the cases," Trey said and looked at him.

"Mariela and I can review the new reports on the inspectors and see why that foundation was scheduled for a reinspection," Ricky said.

"I'll speak to Mia about her friend and see if she thinks he'll assist us," Samantha said, stood and walked away from the table, already phoning Mia with their request.

"I'm heading to the office to see where we stand on our other cases," his father said and likewise rushed away from the room.

"I guess the rest of us should get to work as

well. I'll keep you posted if I hear anything," Trey said and stood to leave.

"Stay safe, *mano*," Ricky said, and Mariela echoed his concern.

Trey jabbed a finger in their direction. "You, too. Just read the reports and leave the rest up to us," he said and left.

Once he had gone, he faced Mariela, cupped her cheek and said, "You know I can't just do that. We need to nail that bastard for all that he's done."

She offered him a pained smile. "I know. I want to see him behind bars as well."

"I'm glad we agree," he said just as his phone pinged. He snuck a peek and said, "The report is here."

Mariela's smile broadened. "Let's get to work."

Chapter Nineteen

Mariela raked her fingers through her hair in frustration and anger at herself as they finished reviewing the report Sophie and Robbie had sent over. "I always had a niggling worry that Jorge was doing something wrong. I should have said something."

"What would he have done to you if he found out you had talked to someone? At least you have us in your corner now," Ricky said, understanding her frustration but obviously concerned about how risky it would have been for her to go it alone.

She smiled and grasped his hand as it rested on the table. "I do have you and your family helping me. You don't know how grateful I am for that."

He held her hand and gave a gentle squeeze. "You have us, and we have connections. *Tia* Elena's law office also does real estate work. Let's call her and see if she can't get us the name of someone we can speak to in the building inspection department."

He made the call and his aunt said she would

check with her colleagues in that department for the name of a friendly contact.

"Thank you, *tia*," he said, stood and rubbed his flat stomach. "I don't know about you, but I'm hungry."

She'd only had the coffee earlier that morning and her stomach warned her with a rumble that it made sense to get something to eat. Especially if they were probably going to leave to chat with someone once his aunt provided a name.

"I am hungry. Do you want to go make some lunch?" she said, pushed to her feet and stretched to work out the kinks from sitting for so long.

Josie and Samantha were in the kitchen going over a grocery list and menus when they arrived.

"I can make you something for lunch, *Señor* Ricky," Josie said with an adoring smile. The young girl obviously had a crush on the handsome younger Gonzalez brother and Mariela was struck with jealousy.

"It's okay. We can make something ourselves," Ricky said and jerked open the door on one of the large Sub-Zero refrigerators.

Mariela peered inside at the fridge packed with all kinds of fresh vegetables, meats and cheeses. "I make a mean frittata," she said and didn't wait for him to haul out a red pepper, container of mushrooms and a bar of Swiss cheese.

Ricky assisted by grabbing the carton with the eggs and a container of half-and-half. At her questioning look, he said, "Makes the eggs creamier." He passed by one counter and snagged an onion from a woven basket.

They worked at one counter and as they did so Ricky called out, "Do you ladies want to join us for lunch?"

Josie laughed nervously and said, "I have to go to class."

Ricky's mother said, "I'm meeting your father at the office for lunch but thank you for the invitation."

With that they chopped and sautéed the vegetables in a large cast-iron skillet, whipped up the half-and-half and eggs to add to them and topped it with slices of Swiss cheese before popping everything beneath the broiler in the oven.

The cooking smells were making her even hungrier while she kept an eye on the frittata to make sure it wouldn't burn.

Ricky took that time to set the table for two and pour them big glasses of iced tea.

Several minutes later Mariela was slicing pieces of the frittata and plating them. She took them inside to the dining area and Ricky joined her.

Silence filled the air as they filled their bellies, but once that initial hunger had been slaked, Ricky said, "Thank you. This is delicious."

Mariela smiled and dipped her head to acknowledge the compliment. "Thank you as well.

You did help, after all, and that half-in-half did make the eggs creamier."

"A trick I learned from one of our other cooks," he said with a grin and forked up the last of the slice on his plate.

She immediately got him another slice and said, "Have you and your family always had cooks and servants?"

Ricky shook his head, so forcefully it sent the longish strands of hair at the top of his head shifting with the motion. "Not at all. In fact, when we were little, my mother really had to work to put food on the table. My dad was in the military and my *abuelo* had just started SBS. It got a little better once my dad finished his service and went to work as a cop. The worries about food stopped but other worries remained."

She understood. "Like if your dad would come home from work."

Ricky nodded and ate some more of his frittata. "Definitely that. It's always been a dangerous job, but even more so now. I'm glad Trey left the force and hope Roni does as well. We could use someone as bright as her in the agency."

Mariela considered his words as she finished her food. With a shrug, she said, "I don't really know Roni, but she strikes me as someone who really loves her job."

"She does, but she surprised us all when she went into the academy after college. She and the

Twins had been friends forever and we never suspected she wanted to be a cop," he admitted and gobbled down the rest of his second slice.

"I never thought I'd go into marketing, but I liked working with people and it seemed to make more sense since I did so well when I was helping Jorge," she admitted and helped Ricky clear off the table and load the dishes into the dishwasher.

They had just finished cleaning when his aunt called.

"I have a phone number for someone you can contact. I was given the number in confidence because this person has seen the news and is very worried," his aunt said.

RICKY UNDERSTOOD THE individual's concerns given that there had been several attempts on their lives so far. "I understand. Thanks for getting the number."

"I'll text it to you," she said and then quickly tacked on, "Stay safe, Ricky. I'm worried about you both."

"We'll be okay," he said and checked the text message once she'd hung up.

"Let's make this call on the patio. I'm a little tired of being cooped up in the house all day," he said.

They walked to the doors leading to the patio, only Ricky hesitated there to search for the security guards patrolling the grounds. Long moments passed, but he didn't see either of the two men.

Fear filled him at the possibility the guards had been neutralized. Besides the two of them, Josie's mom, Alicia, and her cousin Javier were both probably working somewhere either in the house or on the grounds. If a professional had taken out the guards, he wouldn't think twice about hurting them as well.

He handed Mariela his phone and said, "Lock up after me. If I'm not back in five minutes, call 911."

Her eyes widened in surprise as he reached to the small of his back and pulled out the Glock. "Stay here and lock up," he commanded again and cautiously stepped onto the patio.

He waited until she locked the sliders and crept to the far edge of the property past the pool. Peering up and down the side gardens, he didn't see either of the two guards. Luckily his mom's Jaguar was gone as well as Josie's little Mini-Cooper. It eased his mind that he didn't have to worry about them.

He raced up the side yard to the front of the house. The front gate was secure, and nothing seemed out of the ordinary. Rushing down the other side of the property, he finally caught sight of the guards down by the dock in an area that wasn't visible from the patio sliding doors.

Someone had pulled up close to their dock, and

while one of the guards seemed to be providing directions to an apparently lost boater, the other guard stood a few feet back, monitoring the situation and ready to act.

As the boat pulled away from the dock and the two guards resumed their positions on either end of the waterfront area, Ricky slipped the gun back into the holster and returned to the patio doors.

"Everything's okay," he said, and Mariela ripped open the door and threw her arms around him.

"I was so worried," she said, her head buried against his chest.

He wrapped his arms around her, offering comfort until the trembling in her body stopped. "I overreacted when I didn't see the guards."

"You did the right thing. I didn't realize you were armed." When she stepped away, she motioned to his back.

"You asked me to teach you some self-defense the other night. I asked my dad for help. We decided it made sense for me to be able to protect us," he said and flipped a hand in the direction of the outdoor dining area.

"Let's make that call."

He dialed the number and a man answered. "Is this Gonzalez?"

"Ricky Gonzalez. Can I put you on speaker so my partner can hear?" he asked.

A long hesitation followed. "Sure, but no recording. Hernandez will know who I am if he hears my voice."

. A good fact to know. The two men were apparently quite familiar. It surprised him that the man didn't ask who his partner was, and he didn't offer it up. Especially as Mariela grabbed her phone and tapped out a message.

His voice is familiar.

He nodded to confirm he'd seen what she'd written and said, "No problem. Thanks for talking to me. I understand you know Smith and Levy. What are they like?"

"Used to be regular guys like the rest of us. About four or five years back things started to change. First it was just a fancy vacation that none of us could ever have afforded. Then it was other things and most of us wondered what was up, but none of us had any proof," the man said, his voice suddenly hushed as if he was somewhere he feared being overheard.

The sounds of other voices and machinery filtered into the background and Ricky sensed he didn't have much time to get some answers. "But you have proof now?" he asked.

"No proof, not yet anyway," the man said.

"Does it have to do with Hernandez's mid-rise condo building?" Ricky pressed.

"Smith approved the foundation and it all

seemed fine until one of the senior building inspectors got a call. Someone warned us that things weren't right."

"In what way?" Ricky pushed.

The muted noises of people and machinery in the background came again as the man called out to someone, "I'll be there in a sec."

Then he said to Ricky, "I have to go. All I can say is you need to check that foundation and the ground underneath."

That wasn't enough for Ricky since they already had their suspicions about both. "Why hasn't a new inspection been scheduled?" he hounded.

"I don't really know," the man said, and before Ricky could ask another question, the man hung up.

He peered at the phone and then at Mariela. "You said he sounded familiar."

She nodded. "We sometimes had inspectors at our holiday parties. I think he was one of the people who we invited. I should have those lists on my laptop," she said and, without waiting for him, she raced away to get her computer.

He sat at the table, considering what the man had said. That it had only been four or five years since Smith and Levy had apparently gone on the take. The condo embroiled in many of the lawsuits had been built nearly seven years earlier, presumably before the two inspectors had started taking bribes.

Which meant that the issues there could have been caused by normal settling, or worse, that another inspector was also accepting money.

When Mariela returned with her laptop, she brought up the invitation list. "This was the last party I did for Jorge. I filed for divorce just a few months after that."

He wondered what had finally pushed her over the edge to ask for a divorce and why a man like Jorge had even agreed to it. Had it possibly been the rape she'd mentioned earlier? Had she used the possibility of filing a criminal complaint as leverage? As much as he wanted to know more about that, he wouldn't push. He wanted her to be able to share it with him in her own time.

She had been tap-tap-tapping away to pull up the list, but when she looked up from her screen, she seemed to know what he'd been thinking. She immediately avoided his gaze, focused on the screen and said, "There were four inspectors at that party. Williams and Randall, who had come to other parties. Cook, who the other men called Cookie. He was a new hire. The fourth man was Livan Dillon, the 'Old Man.'"

"Do you think that's who was talking to us?" Ricky asked.

Mariela peered upward, as if searching the sky

for answers, and then grudgingly nodded. "I think it was Dillon."

Something bugged him again along the edges of his brain. "Do you know why they called him 'Old Man'?"

Mariela pursed her lips and did a little shrug. "I got the sense he'd been with the department for a lot longer than they had."

Which meant he might have been around when the inspections had been done on the condo with all the problems. "I need to check something in those inspection reports," he said and held his hand out to invite her to join him inside.

Once they were back in the study, he pulled up the reports and searched them to confirm what he'd thought after chatting with the man and hearing Mariela's idea as to his identity.

"What is it, Ricky?" Mariela asked as she sat beside him and scanned the documents he was bringing up.

"Dillon, if that's who it was, says that it was four or five years ago when Smith and Levy seemed to start taking bribes, but that condo we visited was built almost seven years ago and neither of them did any inspections there. Smith wasn't even employed by the department at that time," he said and ran his index finger over the pertinent data in the report.

Mariela's opened her eyes wide. "Maybe Dillon didn't want us to know who he was because he took a bribe on that project."

Ricky nodded and displayed the detailed reports on the condo inspections. Dillon's name wasn't listed on any of the inspections. He muttered a curse and said, "Are you sure it was his voice?"

"There's one way to find out. May I?" she asked and took over the laptop.

MARIELA SEARCHED THE online inspection system and pulled up the address for a recent inspection Dillon had done. She opened another window and located the phone number for the building inspection department.

Since Dillon might recognize Ricky's number if he had caller ID and also might not answer an unknown number, she used her phone to call his office. "Miami Building Inspections," answered a cheery female voice.

"Livan Dillon, please," she said.

"I'm sorry, but Mr. Dillon is out in the field at the moment," the receptionist advised.

"Oh, no. I really need to speak to him. He just did an inspection at my house in Indian Creek and my contractor has some questions for him. Is there any way to reach him?"

"I'm sorry—"

"Please. My husband will be so angry if we can't get this finished today," she pleaded, hoping it would strike a chord with the woman on the other end of the line.

It did. "Let me see if I can't get him on his cell phone."

Mariela turned on her speaker and held her breath, waiting for Dillon to answer.

"Hello. Hello," he said, and Ricky did a little jump at the sound of his voice, recognizing it immediately.

"Livan Dillon?" she asked, just to confirm.

"Yes, this is he. Who is this?" he said, growing impatient.

"It's Mariela Hernandez and Ricky Gonzalez. I think it's time the three of us met face-to-face," she said.

Chapter Twenty

Livan "Old Man" Dillon wasn't really old, Ricky thought. He just had that kind of look that said he'd seen too much of the world. Suffered too much.

"You're going to get us all killed," Dillon hissed and looked around the Little Havana restaurant where they'd agreed to meet. With it being late afternoon, there were only a few people grabbing afternoon coffees from an outside counter. Locals from the prevalence of the *guayabera* shirts and panama hats on the older men.

"You need to tell us what you know about this development," Ricky said and pushed a sheet of paper with the condo building's photo and address in front of the man.

Dillon took one look at it, leaned back in his chair and laid thickly muscled arms across his lean chest. "I didn't have anything to do with these inspections."

"But you know something you're not saying," Mariela said and jabbed a finger at the address.

"This may be where it all starts. Where all our problems, and yours, begin."

The muscles in his arms clenched at her words and Ricky pushed him to answer. "Whatever you tell us may help keep all of us safe."

An unforgiving laugh escaped Dillon, but then he shook his head, and leaned toward them again. Smoothing his hands over the piece of paper, almost like a caress, he said, "My wife had cancer and the treatments weren't covered by our insurance. I didn't know what to do, but I knew that taking a bribe from Hernandez wasn't the answer."

Ricky didn't quite know what to think about his admission. "Hernandez offered you a bribe and you didn't take it?" he asked just to confirm he had understood Dillon's statement correctly.

"I didn't, but a few days later I saw Hernandez handing an envelope to one of our senior inspectors. I didn't need to be a genius to figure out what was going on," he said with a tired shrug of defeated shoulders.

"Why didn't you say something?" Mariela asked.

That shrug came again. "I hadn't been on the job that long and he had a lot of connections. I couldn't afford to lose my job and my medical insurance. Then he offered me money for my wife's treatments, and I broke. I didn't want to lose her."

"What's his name?" Ricky asked, wishing that

with each new revelation it didn't get more and more complicated. Maybe even more and more dangerous.

At Dillon's prolonged silence, he asked again, "What's his name?"

Dillon didn't answer. He just shook his head and looked away until Mariela laid a hand on his arm.

"Your wife, is she okay?" Mariela asked, her voice filled with understanding and compassion.

Tears erupted in his eyes and spilled down his cheeks, but then the first glimmer of joy crept onto his features. "She is. She's been cancer free six years now. It would kill her to know what I did."

Mariela shook her head. "I don't think so. I think she would understand that you loved her so much you'd do anything to help her get better."

Dillon brushed away the tears and did a little bob of his head. "His name is Billy Rooney. He's also the senior building inspector on your ex's mid-rise project."

THE GROUP GATHERED for dinner that night was even larger since Mia had brought John Wilson with her and his tech guru cousins had also come by.

As Ricky watched Mia and John during the meal, he didn't fail to miss the spark of something there, which surprised him. Mia hadn't really been seriously involved with any man since a sudden breakup with a college boyfriend years earlier. Like the social butterfly that she was, she'd flitted from one man to the other, but never for more than a date or two. By his count, she'd had more dates than that with the tech millionaire.

Carolina seemed to sense it as well, judging from the almost sad look on her face. If Mia did get serious with a man, she probably worried that the Twins would be no more. It wasn't an unreasonable assumption since he'd seen more than one woman's relationship change once a man came into the mix.

After coffee and dessert had been served, Wilson said, "Thank you so much for such a lovely meal, *Señora* Gonzalez."

"We should be thanking you for agreeing to assist us with this case, Mr. Wilson," his mother said.

With a little dip of his head, Wilson said, "If you don't mind, I'd like to hear more about what you need from me."

It was Trey who spoke up rather than his father, hinting at the fact that his father was slowly handing over the reins to his oldest son. "I hope you understand that everything we tell you tonight has to remain confidential."

Wilson chuckled, shook his head and peered at Roni as she sat beside her fiancé. "I guess he doesn't remember that I didn't out you during your last investigation."

"He remembers, John. It's just that this one is very close to our hearts since it strikes at our family," Roni said and laid a hand on Trey's shoulder in a show of solidarity.

Wilson peered at Mia from the corner of his eye and nodded. "It's why I keep my people out of the limelight. What can I do to help you?"

"Thank you," Trey said and did a quick rundown on everything they'd learned so far. As he neared the end, he gestured for Ricky to provide the latest information on the corruption of the building inspectors.

"We know of at least three individuals that Hernandez has bribed," he said, omitting mention of Dillon since he empathized with the man's desire to help his sick wife. "One of the projects is already involved in various lawsuits but the issues don't seem life-threatening."

Wilson inched up an eyebrow. "You think one of the other projects is?"

"We have concerns that the mid-size condo development will be structurally unsound and if it is…it could result in a building collapse," Ricky advised.

"Hmm," Wilson said and leaned back in his chair before shooting forward again. He laced his fingers together and said, "These attacks on your family. You think Hernandez is behind them."

"Jorge is my ex. I overheard him talking to someone about a project. He said it was dangerous and a big risk but if the other person did it he'd get his 'blood money.' A lot of money from what I could tell," Mariela explained.

Wilson bounced his hands on the tabletop and remained silent, mulling over the information. "Have you made any progress in confirming Hernandez is behind the attacks?"

"No," Trey admitted, but quickly added, "But a recent homicide was Hernandez's old foreman, and we were able to confirm the foreman was responsible for the first attack on Mariela."

"But not the shootings or road rage?" Wilson challenged.

"We have CCTV footage from various areas but nothing definitive. The BMW visible at the various crime scenes had stolen plates each and every time," Trey explained.

Sophie jumped in with, "We're trying to secure additional footage from a security company that monitors Hernandez's properties."

Wilson remained silent once again, prompting Mia to say, "It's okay if you don't want to help, John. We'd understand."

Wilson shook his head and peered at Mia as he said, "I wasn't lucky enough to have family growing up." He ripped his gaze from hers and glanced at everyone gathered around the table. "But I see how much you all care for each other and for others," he said, finally settling his gaze on Mariela.

"So, you will help, after all?" Mia said, clearly surprised given what had seemed like his earlier reticence.

"I will, although I warn you, he might not fall for it. I already turned him down when he approached me about buying one of his projects and converting it to office space," Wilson said and reached for his nearly empty coffee mug.

"Let me freshen that for you," his mother said, but Wilson raised his hand to stop her.

"No, thanks. Although a Scotch might hit the spot right about now," he confessed.

Trey smiled. "I think we can make that happen."

AFTER THE SCOTCH and detailed plans on their next steps in the investigation, the family had scattered to go home, and Mia had left with Wilson.

"He seemed like a nice man," Mariela said as Ricky and she strolled around the gardens behind his family home.

"I guess," Ricky said with shrug, only she could tell he was less than happy with his sister's involvement with the other man.

"What don't you like about him?" she asked, wondering about his protectiveness. She'd never had the benefit of a sibling to care about her since she was an only child.

Ricky laughed and did a little wag of his head.

"She's my sister, and as my *abuela* always told the Twins, 'Men are dogs.'"

Mariela did a little stutter-step and faced him. "Really. Does that include you, Ricardo Gonzalez? Should I worry about you?"

He had a wry grin on his lips as he cupped her cheek. "Point taken, only I'm not an eccentric millionaire—"

"Just a millionaire," she teased with a roll of her eyes.

"A very eccentric millionaire who keeps a pied-à-terre in the Del Sol for female-only parties," he said, continuing his earlier tirade.

Even she'd heard rumors about Wilson's weirdness from an assortment of internet news sites as well as the local television news channel when it covered one of his parties. But that didn't make them true or harmful.

"You've got to trust Mia's judgment. Roni's as well, apparently," she said, recalling what the other man had said at dinner about not outing Roni during a prior investigation.

"I guess I do. Let's hope he can get access to that construction site," he said, slipped an arm around her waist and gently urged her back into their stroll.

The night couldn't be more perfect, she thought, inhaling the fragrance from a nearby bush of night-blooming jasmine, but a slightly chilly breeze had a damp feel, warning that rain might be on its way. A new moon barely cast light across the lawn, leaving them in intimate shadows. As they neared a small stand of palms that hid them from the guards and anyone in the house, Ricky tugged her there, leaned against a tree and urged her close.

She went willingly, loving the feel of his hard body against her softness and the way his hands swept up to cup her breasts.

"Is this you being a dog?" she teased and rose on tiptoes to brush a quick kiss on his lips.

"Woof," he kidded, his smile bright even in the dim moonlight.

She kissed that smile, exalting in the joy of it that kindled hope in her heart. His hands moving on her, caressing the sensitive tips of her breasts, kindled passion until she moaned into his mouth.

"Let's go in," Ricky said, and they hurried back to the house and up to his room. But unlike the night before, they didn't dawdle with drinks or conversation. By the time they reached the bed in the center of the room they were naked, and Ricky was reaching into the nightstand to whip out a strip of condoms he'd had a local pharmacy discreetly deliver earlier that day.

She raised her eyebrows at the length of the strip. "Feeling very lucky?"

IT DAWNED ON Ricky then that she often used humor as a defense mechanism when she might be feeling uncomfortable. Like now. He could have joked right back at her, only he wanted to chip away at those defenses to know more about her.

"No, it's not that. This isn't just about getting you into bed. It's about…more."

His words had a totally unexpected result: she shut down as if someone had tossed a bucket of cold water on her.

Rushing to her clothes scattered around the room, she hugged them to her body as if they were a shield.

He chased after her and grabbed her arm when she would have run.

"Don't," she shouted and jerked out of his grasp.

"Tell me what's wrong, Mariela? Tell me why you're running," he said, hands outstretched in pleading.

"You think this is something serious, but what do you really know about me?" she shot back.

"I know you're bright. Intelligent. Brave," he said, recalling what she'd said earlier about how her ex had raped her.

Tears glistened in her eyes and teetered precariously on her thick eyelashes. "How can you even look at me like that when you know what he did to me? That I'm damaged goods."

Her words explained so much. As the tears finally spilled down her cheeks, he swiped them away with the back of his hand. "No one is perfect and sometimes it's those imperfections that make something special. Like you."

MARIELA WANTED TO say that he was perfect, but she'd seen his cracks. "Like the way you worry you aren't as strong as the rest of the men in your family."

His lips thinned to knife-sharp slash and he tipped his head. "Like that. We're two imperfect people, but together…we're a hell of a team."

She didn't try to deny that. Dropping the clothes she'd had in a stranglehold, she took hold of his hand and guided him to the bed. Together they crawled in and beneath the covers. Embracing him, she said, "I want to tell you everything."

HE PACED BACK and forth in his workshop, angry that he hadn't been able to run them into the waters of Biscayne Bay. Now they were holed up even more tightly at the Gonzalez family compound.

Since it would be impossible to get past the security gate off the causeway, he'd tried to sneak in via the canal only to find two armed guards patrolling the waterfront. They'd chased him away quickly, not buying his story that he'd gotten lost on his way to a friend's home on the island.

He was going to have to bide his time to try to hit at them again. In the meantime, he'd keep a close eye on them, although he suspected that they would try and find a way to visit one of the new developments.

He'd be waiting for them when they did.

Chapter Twenty-One

They'd stayed up for hours as she'd shared more about what had happened during her marriage. He'd listened, but as a lover and not a psychologist. When she'd emptied her heart of so many fears and doubts, he'd shared his own and found togetherness with that giving.

Exhausted, they'd fallen to sleep but woken to make love.

As the first fingers of dawn had crept into the room, she'd roused him with her caresses and kisses and they'd made love again, welcoming a new day and maybe even a new beginning between them.

They'd taken a quick shower—together—and rushed down for breakfast. Ricky's mother was already there, reading the morning paper. Trey as well, devouring a large plate of pancakes and bacon.

"You keep eating like that and you'll never fit in your tux for the wedding," Ricky teased.

"Don't worry. I'm going to work it off," Trey said with a knowing glance between the two of them.

"Whatever you do with Roni is TMI, *mano*," Ricky parried to deflect from them.

"It is. Apologies," his older brother said and clearly meant it.

"Can I get you a *café con leche*?" his mother asked.

"I'd love some. Thanks," Mariela said, and luckily Josie came in a second later with two plates piled high with pancakes and bacon. She placed them in front of their seats and said, "I'll bring some hot maple syrup in a second."

"Thank you," she said just as Samantha handed her a mug and returned to her seat.

"Your father went in early to work on some things. What's on your list for today?" Ricky's mother asked Trey.

His brother stopped slicing up his pancakes and said, "Hounding the detectives to see if they have anything new on the attacks and talk to the ME to see if he has anything else. I'm hoping that rope had some DNA on it that will lead us to Hernandez."

Trey forked up some of his pancake and paused with it halfway to his mouth. "You two are going to stay in touch with Wilson and Mia, right?"

Ricky nodded. "We are. Hopefully Hernandez will agree to Wilson visiting the site."

"But will Wilson see anything more than just the cracks we've heard about?" Mariela asked as

Josie returned with the promised maple syrup. She smiled at the young woman and thanked her.

"I don't know Wilson well, but I suspect he'll do a thorough visual inspection. I should get going," Trey said and took a final bite of his breakfast.

He was about to walk out when his phone rang. "What's up, Soph?"

Listening for just a few minutes, Trey said, "Hold on and let me put you on speaker."

Sophie's voice burst through the line. "Robbie and I know Wilson is hoping to visit the site today, but we had an idea."

"Go ahead, Josefina," Samantha said, using Sophie's given name.

"It seems as if there's worry about the ground settling where it shouldn't be. We could use lidar to map the topography at the site and see just how much it's settled. Even do projections of what might happen when it does," she said.

"How does that work?" Trey asked and sat back down.

"We'd have to send up a drone to get some information and then analyze it with software," Robbie explained.

"Wouldn't the construction crew see a drone flying over them?" Mariela said, thinking that she'd seen one flying over more than once to get photos and video for their marketing.

"We'd send it up at night. It can actually be better for the laser at night and there's generally less air traffic as well," Sophie said.

Trey looked around the table, gauging their reactions before he said, "Please get ready to do it."

"Will do. In the meantime, we'll finish up what we can on the CCTV and webcam images," Robbie advised, and the line went dead as he hung up.

"It sounds like a great idea," Ricky said, grateful for his techie cousins and their skills.

"I guess we just wait for their report and Wilson," Mariela said, slightly disheartened that there wasn't more that she could do to help.

"You've done a lot, Mariela. All your connections helped us get to this point," Ricky said, reading her like the proverbial open book.

"He's right. We know as much as we do thanks to you," Trey agreed.

"Thank you," she said, but despite their words, guilt lingered that they were at risk because of what she'd overheard and her psycho husband.

It made her lose her appetite despite how wonderful the pancakes had tasted. "I think I need some air."

When Ricky rose to go with her, she stopped him with an upraised hand and nearly ran from the room.

"She feels responsible," his mother said as she stared at Mariela fleeing the room.

"If she hadn't overheard and been brave enough

to do something about it, people might have died," Ricky said.

"Even if you do the right thing, you still feel the guilt," Trey said and leaned heavily on his chair.

His brother had always been the strong silent type, but for the first time Ricky was seeing a crack in that tough exterior. "You still feel responsible about your partner's death."

Trey gripped the top rung of the chair so hard his fingers went white with the pressure. "We did the right thing to investigate. I did all I could to get to him. To save him, only…"

It hadn't been enough, Ricky thought as Trey rushed from the room.

"I'm an idiot." His job was to read people and yet with two people he cared about he hadn't been able to see what was right in front of his face.

"Love can blind you sometimes," his mother said, as intuitive as ever.

"I'm not sure I'm in love with her." There was so much happening, and he worried that it was too soon.

His mother gave an exasperated sigh and rose to clear off the table. While she did so, she said, "You've always been my planner, my responsible one. You can't plan love, Ricardo. It just kind of happens."

She didn't wait for him to respond and left him sitting there, staring at the empty table and the remnants of his breakfast. Pieces of pancake drowned in a gloppy mess of melted butter and maple syrup.

In a way, he was drowning a little, too. Much like his mother had pointed out, he'd always been the one who'd needed structure and safety. If he had to psychoanalyze himself, it was possibly because of his family's unsettled years when he'd been little. He'd never wanted a life like his father's. He'd wanted stability, and yet here he was, embroiled in a situation as dangerous as any that his father or brother had ever been in.

"Ricky?" Mariela said as she returned to the table, her emerald gaze dark with worry.

"I was just thinking about all we had to do today," he lied, not wanting to add to her guilt.

If she saw through his fib, she didn't say. "Maybe we should see what we can find out about Rooney?" she said, referring to the senior inspector that Dillon had mentioned.

"That's a good idea. I don't think I could just sit here and wait," he said, hopped up from the table and grabbed his dish to take it into the kitchen.

At his action, a flicker of a smile flashed across her lips.

Puzzled, he narrowed his gaze in question and she gestured to the plates in his hands. "Your mom taught you well."

He grinned and nodded. His very perceptive mom had taught him that and more. "She most certainly did." As he placed the plates near the sink where his mother was rinsing the dishes, he dropped a kiss on her cheek.

"Just because," he said at her quizzical look and returned to the dining area where Mariela waited, still smiling.

She held her hand out to him and he twined his fingers with hers and walked with her into the other room. They'd been pulled into this situation together and together they would find a way out of it.

MARIELA WATCHED AS RICKY, Trey and their cousins tested the drone in the backyard.

Sophie was operating the controls while Robbie monitored the path of the drone on his laptop. Trey and Robbie stood across the way from them, heads bent together as they chatted.

"We used satellite views of this property and the construction site to program the drone's route," Sophie explained to her as the drone took flight. It hovered in the air directly above them and she said, "You can run the program now, Robbie."

Sophie's brother tapped a few keys and the drone started flying back and forth across the property for the family home, gathering information.

The drone had something that looked like a small camera in the middle, facing downward. Mariela pointed to it and asked, "Is that the laser thing?"

Sophie nodded and smiled. "It is. The laser will take measurements, and once we have that, we'll use software to map the ground. We can even strip away any vegetation and man-made structures to see what it looks like."

"Amazing," Mariela said, watching the drone zip back and forth across the sky.

"What's amazing is what they're discovering with lidar, like whole Mayan cities and Egyptian pyramids," Robbie added from beside them as he kept an eye on the computer.

Trey and Ricky had been watching as well from across the yard, but seeing that the drone was working just fine, they joined Mariela and the cousins.

"Looks like it's working great," Ricky said.

"You've got the construction site programmed the same way?" Trey asked as he leaned over Robbie to view the laptop screen.

"We do. We got a satellite view of the site and programmed it. We can launch from the parking lot of the condo building next to it," Sophie advised.

"Great work. The three of us will go once it's totally dark," Trey said, but Ricky and she immediately protested.

"We're going as well," she said.

Ricky agreed. "We're in this because of us so we're going."

Trey jammed his hands on his hips and his

shoulders shifted with his very visible harrumph. But then they drooped with resignation as he said, "I get it. I don't have to like it, but I get it."

His mother stepped out from the house and called out, "Come in and get something to eat."

"Because nothing gets you ready for an assignment like a full stomach," Trey teased with a chuckle.

"It's a sign of love, *mano*," Ricky said and clapped his brother on the back.

Robbie hopped to his feet, inhaled deeply and wrung his hands together in anticipation. "It smells like *picadillo*. Your mom makes a mean *picadillo*."

He rushed off toward the house, leaving them all chuckling and following at a slower pace.

Inside, Robbie had already plopped himself at the table and his mother and Josie were bringing out big platters with rice and the *picadillo* Robbie had salivated over.

Mariela smiled and sat, relishing the comfort that came from sharing a meal with family.

There was genial teasing as Robbie piled his plate high with rice and the meat flavored with tomato sauce, onions, peppers, garlic and olives. "You make the best *picadillo*, *tia*," he said.

"Thank you, Robbie. That's high praise because your mom is quite a cook," Samantha said.

"When she isn't busy cooking up some weird program," Trey said around a mouthful of food.

The comment puzzled Mariela. "Your mom is a programmer?"

Sophie shook her head and swallowed. "Kind of. She and my dad work for the NSA."

"Wow, the NSA? Like supersecret spy types?" Mariela said, eyes wide in surprise.

"Kind of," Sophie said again with a little lift of her shoulders.

"If we told you what they really did we'd have to kill you," Robbie teased, but Mariela suspected that maybe it wasn't all that far from the truth.

"*Tia* Mercedes is my dad's sister. He always says she's the smartest Gonzalez," Ricky said with a grin.

Considering how impressive all the Gonzalez family members were, Mercedes had to be a genius, but then again, she probably was a genius since she was working for the NSA.

The family continued chatting, explaining how Mercedes had met her husband as well as how Samantha and Ramon had met. Which left her wondering about Carolina's connection and Ricky explained.

"Carolina and Pepe, whose real name is Jose, are my *tio* Jose's kids. He's my dad's younger brother. Mercedes is the baby sister."

"So many family members," she said, her mind whirling with all the names.

Ricky patted her hand in understanding. "Don't worry. You'll get to meet them all eventually."

"I'm looking forward to it," she said, optimistic that whatever was happening with Ricky would continue after the conclusion of the investigation.

They were halfway through the meal when Ricky's father finally showed up, looking a little tired and worn.

"Everything okay?" Samantha asked as she rose and dropped a kiss on his cheek.

"Fine, just a small problem," he said, slipped off his suit jacket and took his spot at the head of the table.

"Anything I can help with?" Trey immediately asked, bringing a smile to his father's face.

"In time, *mi' jo*," his father said and dug into the plate that his wife placed in front of him.

Dinner resumed at a leisurely pace, especially since they had to wait for full night to fall in order to fly the drone. They had just finished the meal with coffee and flan when Trey peered out the window to the darkness beyond.

"It's time," he said.

Chapter Twenty-Two

They had no issue pulling into the parking lot for the condo building next to Hernandez's construction site and Sophie and Robbie had the drone up in no time.

Ricky tracked the small flashing red and white lights as it ran his cousin's program to map the topography of the ground. Mariela stood next to him, but her gaze was fixed not on the drone, but on the building behind them.

"I don't see any cracks on this building," she said, and both Trey and he turned to scrutinize the structure.

After a long inspection, Ricky said, "I don't either, but maybe it's possible the ground here is more stable."

"Or they did remedial work to stabilize it," Trey said, which reminded Ricky of something the condo owners involved in the lawsuit had said.

"Those condo owners said Hernandez didn't want to do that because it was too expensive," he repeated.

"And we've heard that he's strapped for cash," Mariela added.

"We'll see just how bad the situation is once we have the footage and can analyze it," Sophie said over her shoulder, but her gaze was fixed on the drone.

From what Ricky could see, the drone was half-way over the property, and it hadn't been all that long, maybe fifteen minutes. Which made him wonder aloud, "How long will it take to analyze the data you get?"

Sophie made a face. "That's the rub. It could take up to twenty-four hours to process on our computers."

"What about on Wilson's computers?" Trey asked.

"He's probably got some kind of supercom-puter to run all his programs. I'm thinking a few hours?" Sophie said.

"You're going to ask him for another favor?" Ricky said, worried by what all those favors were going to do to his sister's budding relationship with the wealthy tech mogul.

Trey did a little shrug. "Yeah, I get where you're going. We can wait. Wilson isn't going to inspect the property until tomorrow anyway. Hernandez is apparently playing it cool and making it seem like there's no rush to sell it off."

"Almost done," Robbie said, but a second later a series of gunshots rang out in the night.

"Damn. They're shooting at the drone," Trey said.

"Just a few more passes," Sophie said and focused on Robbie's laptop, watching the progress.

Trey shot his arm out in the direction of their SUV. "Load up any loose gear and get in the car," he instructed and raced over to grab the case for the drone.

He joined his brother to lift the large carrying case for the device into the back of the SUV while Mariela picked up a smaller duffel with supplies the cousins had also brought with them.

Voices called out in the dark, the words muted until someone shouted out, "Take down that drone."

A volley of gunfire erupted, shooting up at the drone.

"I'm bringing it home," Sophie said as Robbie stood and started walking toward the SUV with the laptop. "I've got the data," he confirmed.

In a few seconds Sophie had landed the drone and they were lifting it into the back of the SUV.

The heavy pounding of footsteps getting closer sounded from the other side of the fence, but by then they were all in the car and pulling away.

As Ricky peered over his shoulder toward the fence, a head popped over for the barest second, but not long enough for him to see much of anything.

"I think you made a clean getaway," he said, but as they were about to pull out of the entrance to the condo, a black SUV blocked their path and armed guards jumped out.

Trey immediately put the car in reverse and drove backward until with a sharp turn that sent all of them flying side to side in their seats he whipped out of a service entrance for the building.

As he did so Ricky looked back, hoping they weren't being followed. Luckily, a trio of police cruisers had boxed in the black SUV and the security guards stood there, hands raised above their heads.

Trey took a quick look at the rearview mirror. "Someone must have called in the gunshots."

"Thank God," Mariela said from beside them. "They were going to shoot us."

Trey shook his head. "I don't think so. They probably only wanted the drone."

"We still would have had the data. It was feeding to a cloud account," Robbie said.

"But they would have guessed that we knew something was wrong with that property. And Hernandez was willing to kill Mariela for just that reason," Ricky pointed out, and beside him Mariela shook with fear.

"I'm sorry I got you all involved in this," she said again.

"Stop apologizing. You did the right thing. You could be saving lives," Trey said, rising anger in his voice.

"Chill, Trey," Ricky warned as Mariela's body

trembled beside his and he slipped his arm to pull her close and comfort her.

"Sorry. I'm just frustrated at how long it's taking. I want you all to be safe and I know we'll make it happen," he said, hands tight on the steering wheel.

"We'll start processing the data immediately and let you know as soon as we have the info," Sophie said, trying to ease Trey's frustration.

"I know you will, Soph. You guys have been amazing through all this," Trey said and glanced at them in the rearview mirror. "You and Mariela also. It's thanks to all of you that we're this close to nailing Hernandez," he said and held one hand up with his index finger and thumb just an inch apart to emphasize his words.

Ricky knew part of his frustration was also that the detectives handling the cases had found little evidence at any of the scenes. "Did you hear anything from the ME yet?" he asked, hoping there was a least some motion on that front.

"He has some DNA off the rope, but no match against any databases," Trey said.

"But it could be Jorge's, right?" Mariela asked, likewise beginning to show some frustration.

"It could. The detectives asked him for a sample when they went to question him about Ramirez, but he lawyered up and we don't really have enough for a warrant," Trey said as he pulled onto the highway for the ride back to their family home.

"What about a genealogy site? Jorge did one of those a few years ago," Mariela said.

"Also need a warrant," Trey confirmed.

"Any family who's pissed off at him?" Ricky asked, thinking they might be able to at least do a familial match.

"He's an only child," Mariela offered up.

"I guess we have to wait on that until we have more," Ricky said and didn't miss how his brother's hands tightened on the wheel of the car.

Sophie reached over to squeeze Trey's shoulder in reassurance. "We'll have more soon," she said.

"We will," Trey said, but it was almost as if to convince himself.

Mariela slipped her hand into Ricky's, looked up at him and mouthed, *It'll be okay.*

He smiled, bent and dropped a kiss on her lips, whispering, "It will."

The rest of the drive passed in silence, everyone lost in their thoughts. When they opened the gate and pulled into the courtyard in front of the house, a bright red Lamborghini was parked off to one side.

"Sweet Lord, do you know what that is? It's a Veneno," Robbie said in awe when they pulled up beside the supercar. "It costs a few million," he said and hopped out to inspect the Lamborghini.

"I guess Wilson's here," Trey said in amusement.

"I guess so," Ricky said and climbed out of the SUV to examine the über-pricey automobile.

Trey jammed his hands on his hips and scoffed as he looked at the car. "Overcompensating much."

Sophie barely shot a glance at the car and said, "Boys and their toys."

Mariela grabbed hold of his hand and playfully pulled him away from the shiny red toy. "Let's go see why Mia and John are here."

Reluctantly, he said, "You're right."

Inside Mia and John were sitting at the dining area table with his mother and father, having coffee.

His father rose, worry etching deep lines on his face. "The police scanner said there was gunfire at your location."

"The guards shot at the drone and then came after us, but Trey was able to get us away," Ricky said and tossed a hand in the direction of his brother and cousins, who had just come through the door.

"Armed guards seem a little extreme at a construction site," Wilson said with the lift of a light brown brow.

"It does and it might make it harder for you to inspect the location," Ricky said.

"You said they shot at a drone. With lidar, I assume," Wilson said and glanced toward Sophie and Robbie.

Sophie nodded and took a spot at the table. "We

plan to map the topography of the site to see if there is sinking going on."

"We'll also strip away the building and any other structures or vegetation to see what's happening there," Robbie added.

"Impressive. You must need a lot of computing power for that," Wilson said with a quick dip of his head.

The cousins shared a look that the tech millionaire immediately understood. "If it would help, I have a supercomputer that we've put together for a new venture. I'd be more than happy to help out."

"That would really speed things up," Sophie said with a grateful sigh.

Wilson reached into the pocket of his white linen shirt, extracted a business card and handed it to them. "This is my number and also one for Miles, my half brother. He's my business partner. Let him know you're sending the data and we'll process it immediately."

"Thank you, John," Mia said. She was sitting beside him, but judging from her body language, Ricky sensed all was not right with her and Wilson. In truth, Ricky was wondering why the man was being so accommodating when he barely knew the family.

Trey must have also been getting those vibes since he said, "We're really grateful, but—"

Wilson raised a hand to stop him. "It's too much. I get it. Most people would believe I want something in return," he said and shot a look at Mia from the corner of his eye.

His sister tensed even more, and the lines of her beautiful face grew hard.

"I don't, but if one day I need help, I hope you'd do the same," he said.

An uneasy silence filled the air until Trey said, "We would. You just have to ask."

Wilson smiled, his hazel eyes bright and without deception if Ricky was a good judge.

"I hope I won't have to ask," he said without hesitation.

"Are you ready for your visit tomorrow?" his father asked, worry still sitting heavily on his face and in the tightness of his body. It concerned Ricky because his father rarely wore his emotions on his sleeve, but since his arrival last night, something had clearly been troubling him. He'd have to get him aside and ask, not that he thought his father would share.

"I am, only I'm not so sure that a visual inspection will tell you much. What you really need, besides what Sophie and Robbie are doing, is to see what's underground," Wilson said.

"You mean ground penetrating radar?" Sophie said, her mind clearly racing with ideas.

Wilson nodded, but Trey immediately said, "I doubt Hernandez will let you do that if he knows there's an issue."

"You're right. He seemed eager for me to take

the property as is, no questions asked. That alone is a red flag," Wilson said, and everyone around the table nodded in agreement.

MARIELA PROCESSED ALL that Wilson had said, but something just didn't seem right to her. "Jorge was willing to bribe someone to let that building go up. Now he's selling it? Why? To avoid paying the bribe?"

"Or to avoid something that even he thinks is too dangerous to do," Ricky offered.

With all that she knew about her husband, and the way he'd treated her, she found that altruism too hard to believe. "Maybe, only that's not the Jorge I know."

"There's only one way to find out. After I take a look around, I'll tell him I'm not interested in the property," Wilson said.

Chapter Twenty-Three

"I thought he'd stroke out. Red face, eyes bulging," Wilson said and emphasized it with his hands the following day.

"Jorge has a temper," Mariela added as the team sat at the outside dining area to shade themselves from the midday sun.

"He does, but we have some really good news," his father said, looking a little more relieved than he had last night. "I gave *Tio* Jose all the information we'd gathered. It wasn't easy, but I convinced him to open an investigation into the building inspection department."

"That is good news," Ricky said, guessing that the tension he'd sensed had been caused by conflict between the two brothers. Even though he was relieved about his father, he wondered why Mia hadn't come with Wilson to share what had happened that morning at the construction site.

"But will they be watching Jorge in time to catch him paying the bribe?" Mariela said and raked her fingers through the waves of her caramel-colored hair.

His father pursed his lips and said, "I'm not sure."

So close and yet still so very far, Mariela thought, her gut tightening with worry that, despite everything, her ex was going to get away with what he had done and what he planned to do.

"We have to do more," she said softly, that worry driving her to speak out. "What about that radar John mentioned?"

"The problem is getting on-site because of those armed guards," Trey said, but she could tell ideas were already spinning around in his brain on how to do it.

"A decoy," Ricky said, almost as if reading his brother's brain.

"The drone," Sophie added, totally in sync with her cousins.

"We can send it up and pull the guards away from the site so we can use the radar to do some testing," Robbie said.

"I can ask around and see if we can get the radar," Wilson said, but Trey was quick to shut him down.

"We appreciate everything you've done, John, but I can't ask you to do something that risky."

With a shrug, Wilson relented. "I understand.

I'll send over that lidar data ASAP. It should be ready soon," he said and rose from the table.

Trey, Ricky and their dad stood as well and shook the other man's hand. "We really do appreciate it," Ricky said, and the others echoed his words.

"*No problema.* I guess I'll see you around," Wilson said and walked away, leaving Mariela to wonder if things with him and Mia hadn't worked out. Especially since she hadn't come with him, and Mariela had sensed tension the night before.

Once he was gone, everyone sat back down around the table and started planning. She sat back, listening. It was like watching generals mapping out a military campaign as Trey and his father laid out the primary objective while Ricky, Sophie and Robbie tossed out suggestions.

She was impressed as Ricky held his own with the others because this really wasn't his thing. Even though he occasionally helped the agency, he was a psychologist with his own work and life.

She felt a little useless just sitting there, but there wasn't any more that she could add to the conversation. But as they started laying out the responsibilities for all that they would have to do that night, she piped in with, "I'm going as well. I have no intention of just sitting here, waiting and worrying."

Trey raised his hands to quiet her, but Ricky

said, "She's as much a part of this as the family, maybe more."

"I am," she said, appreciating his support.

With that, they worked together to complete the plans for breaking into the site that night.

He looks dangerously sexy in all black, Mariela thought as Ricky finished dressing. It made his chestnut brown hair look even darker and his light blue eyes pop. His black eye and the bruises around his face were finally fading and the first hints of evening stubble shaded his cheeks and chin, making him look even sexier.

She walked up to him and cradled his cheek, rubbing her hands across the sandpapery stubble. He laid a hand on her waist and drew her close. "You don't have to do this," he said and leaned his forehead against hers.

"I have to. I have to make sure he gets the justice he deserves," she said and tilted her head to drop a butterfly-light kiss on his lips.

When she pulled away, he tightened his hand at her waist and kissed her hard, deepening the kiss until they were straining against each other despite making love just an hour earlier.

A cough jerked them apart.

Trey stood at the door, eyeing them with concern. "It's time to go. Are you sure you want to do this?"

Mariela met Ricky's gaze and he said, "We're sure."

"Then let's roll," Trey said and tapped the door-jamb in emphasis before whirling to hurry down the stairs.

Ricky slipped his arm around her waist, and they followed Trey to the dining area where Sophie had placed several printouts on the table. Robbie stood beside the table with his laptop in hand. Ricky's mother and father sat tensely, a radio and laptop in front of them.

"These are the renderings that we were able to create from the lidar data we got from the drone," Sophie explained and ran her fingers along what looked like topographical maps.

"There is unusual unsettling all along this area and beneath the building," Robbie said as Sophie pointed out the areas on the maps. "We were also able to calculate the rate at which the building was settling and what might happen," he added and flipped open his computer to run the simulation.

They watched as the simulation showed the gradual lean of one side of the building until it got so severe that half of the structure completely sheered off the rest of the building and collapsed onto the ground.

"That could kill a lot of people," Ricky said with a low whistle.

"I know Jorge is desperate, but to do something like this…" Mariela said, anger and disgust in her tone.

"It's why we have to stop him," Ricky said and hugged her to his side.

Trey gestured to the maps. "We want to use the GPR on those areas in the simulation to see what's happening underground. Ricky and I will run the radar. Mariela will be our lookout."

He peered from Sophie to Robbie. "Are you two sure you can use the drone to draw away the security guards?"

"As long as you got us a good driver, we can lure them away," Sophie said, no hesitation in her voice.

Mariela wished she could be as certain. "Will we have a driver as well?"

"You will. I've pulled in two of the best drivers from the South Beach Security pool. Roni will also be available in case we need help," Trey confirmed and gestured to the radio and laptop in front of his parents. "*Mami* and *papi* will be tracking the cars and communications in case we need to call in Roni and her police colleagues."

Murmurs drifted around the table from everyone and then Ricky asked, "What do we do next?"

"Let me get you all wired up with the coms so we can stay in touch," Trey said and walked over with a large black suitcase that he laid on the table. He opened it, pulled out communications equipment and got everyone prepared. Once they'd confirmed that everyone could communicate, including with Ricky and Trey's parents, they flew into action.

Trey almost jogged down the few stairs from the front door to the courtyard where two SUVs waited along with the two drivers Trey had mentioned earlier. In a flurry of activity, Mariela piled into the vehicle with Ricky and Trey, and they drove off, the other SUV trailing behind them.

HE WATCHED THEM pull away from the Gonzalez family compound in the two black SUVs. From what he could see through the gate, two of the heirs to the agency were in the SUV in the lead, heading to the construction site, he guessed.

He was ready for them. More than ready thanks to a guard who was willing to look the other way for a nice wad of money.

He smiled as he imagined tripping the surprise he had in the building. Watching it all come down around the Gonzalez family members.

Putting down the binoculars, he wheeled his car around and onto the causeway to head to the site, careful to keep a discreet distance from the two SUVs.

Minutes later, one of the SUVs peeled away, but he kept his eyes on the prize: the SUV carrying the Gonzalez heirs.

It traveled to within a few blocks of the site and pulled over.

He doubled back toward the construction location and parked, gleefully anticipating the moment when he'd teach them all a lesson.

"WHENEVER YOU'RE READY, SOPHIE," Trey said from the front passenger seat.

Ricky tightened his hold on Mariela's hand, anxious about the plan they had all agreed on. It seemed like there were too many things that had to fall into place for them to accomplish their mission.

Across the earpiece he wore, Sophie said, "I'm sending the drone up over the site now. Robbie has hacked their CCTV to confirm if any guards are left on the site."

"Roger that. Let us know when we can go in," Trey instructed.

"Will do," Sophie said, and Ricky sucked in a breath, his heart pounding as he waited for the moment they'd have to head onto the location.

Long minutes passed and he tapped his foot nervously until Mariela laid a hand on his knee. "*Mi amor*, I think I can hear your knees knocking."

"Nervous," he admitted and twined his fingers with hers.

"Me, too. It feels like the wait is forever—"

"It's time to go. Robbie says all the guards have gone to follow them," Trey said, and with a tap on the dashboard, the driver shot the SUV forward and down the few blocks to the entrance to the construction site.

The security guards had left the gate open in their haste to chase after the drone and whoever was controlling it.

As Ricky exited the SUV, he caught sight of the red and white lights on the drone flying away from the construction lot. Sophie and Robbie had done their part; now they had to do theirs.

He rushed to the rear of the SUV where Trey and he muscled the radar device out of the back of the vehicle. The GPR was larger than a lawn mower and a lot heavier, but still manageable between them. Once it was on the ground, Trey called out to the driver, "Turn the car around so we can make a fast exit."

Mariela stood beside them, hands wrapped around the binoculars they'd given her to use.

Ricky looked at the shell of the building that had already been constructed. "You should be able to be a lookout from the third floor."

He bent to give her a quick kiss and she was off, rushing toward the structure.

"Let's move this into place," Trey said, and together they pushed the GPR device toward the edge of the building, which the lidar had identified as having the most settling.

Once they had it in place, his brother said, "I hope I remember how to get this working."

The contact who had lent them the device had

provided them a quick lesson earlier that afternoon and Ricky was sure of how to get it running. "Let me," he said and urged his brother aside.

With the press of a few buttons, the device jumped to life and Ricky slowly pushed it along the edge, collecting the data they would need to know whether what was happening belowground could cause the collapse of the building that Sophie and Robbie had predicted in their simulation.

His hands were damp on the handles, his heartbeat racing as he focused on the task. Run the GPR device too fast and they wouldn't get accurate data. But with every second that passed they ran the risk of the armed security guards returning and it was anyone's guess what would happen then.

Steadying his breath and his pace, he pushed on, intent on finishing the task.

MARIELA HAD ENTERED the shell of the building and found a staircase that she used to race up to the third floor of the partially constructed structure. There was only one other floor above, but the plans she remembered seeing on the real estate listing had shown at least two more floors. As she ran up the stairs, her flashlight providing light, she looked for signs of damage to the structure, but couldn't see any since the staircase was on the side of the building farthest from the area where the settling was occurring.

When she reached the third floor, she shut off the flashlight, pulled out the binoculars and searched for the drone and the SUV with Sophie and Robbie as well as the other black SUV with the guards from the building site. Neither was in sight, giving her some peace of mind that they'd have more than enough time to finish their testing of the ground before having to make an escape.

She walked to the opposite side of the building and flipped on the flashlight, careful to shield its light with her body while she inspected the areas around the support columns. Sure enough, there were small hairline cracks already developing just as her ex's foreman had warned.

She hurried to the next column and noted the same kind of damage. She was about to shut off the flashlight when from the corner of her eye something caught her attention. Training the flashlight on the column near the stairs, she noticed a blob plastered to the base of the column. Inching closer, she realized there were several blobs pressed against all the columns in that row. Wires ran from one to the other and as she tracked them down she realized they all led to a small box with a red LED indicator.

2:58, the LED said.

2:57.

2:56.

Her heart stopped dead. A bomb. And there

was only a little less than three minutes before it would go off.

"Trey. Ricky. There's a bomb on the third floor. We only have a little over two and a half minutes to get out of here before it blows," she said and raced toward the staircase.

For a moment, Ricky imagined that he hadn't just heard what Mariela had said.

"Repeat, Mariela. Did you say a bomb?" Trey asked as Ricky finished a pass along the building's edge and turned to do another.

"Bomb. Two minutes. Boom," Mariela said, her breath short and choppy across the line.

Trey called to the driver. "Get ready to roll," he commanded, and the SUV's engine roared to life.

"Come on, Ricky. Shut that thing down," Trey said, but Ricky had to finish the pass, worried that if they didn't they wouldn't have enough data to confirm their fears.

"I have to finish," he said, maintaining his pace even though his flight response was saying to get the hell out of there.

Trey peered at his watch. "We've only got a little more than a minute," he warned just as Mariela rushed over to them.

"We've got to go," she urged Ricky, but he didn't waver, taking the last almost painfully slow steps to finish the pass.

"Let's go," he shouted and shut down the radar.

Together the three of them picked up the GPR device, hauled it over to the SUV and almost tossed it into the back.

They jumped into the vehicle and the driver sped away just as the first boom sounded and was followed by three other blasts.

The ground shook beneath them, but the driver steadied the car, and they flew out of the construction lot and into the street as a loud rumble filled the air.

As they drove a safe distance away, Trey, Ricky and Mariela turned in their seats to see the one side of the building coming down and crashing onto the ground, the force of the blasts and the collapse strong enough to shake their SUV and trip the car alarms of several vehicles in the area.

It took only seconds for the sounds of sirens to join the wail of the car alarms and Roni's voice shot across their earpieces.

"Trey, are you all okay?"

"We are, but you need to get here. Someone set off a bomb," he said.

THE POLICE HAD questioned them at the site and then taken them over to the nearest precinct where Roni, *Tio* Jose and *Tia* Elena had come to help them during the interviews the detectives assigned to the investigation had wanted to conduct.

They had provided all the details they had about the bribes and the attacks on their lives, only omitting the names of Hernandez's current foreman and Dillon. His uncle had confirmed to the police that his office already had all the details and were commencing their own investigation of the building inspectors and Hernandez.

Seemingly satisfied, the detectives were about to release them when they received a call from the police officers investigating the other earlier attacks.

"Let me put you on speakerphone," the one officer said and peered around the room at the various Gonzalez members gathered around the interview table.

"Please give us your report," the detective requested.

"We went to Hernandez's home to advise him about the incident at his construction site, but no one answered. When we did a quick inspection, we noticed that someone was in a front room and attempted to get a response again. When there wasn't one, we entered."

Ricky's gut clenched as he waited and wrapped an arm around Mariela, expecting the worst.

In a forced, almost clinical monotone, the detective said, "We found a male inside with a gunshot wound to the head. We identified him as Jorge Hernandez, but we'll need someone to come and identify him at the ME's."

Mariela sucked in a shocked breath and whispered, "I'll go ID but it can't be Jorge. He would never do something like that."

The detective on the line continued with his report. "We searched the home for any signs of forced entry, but there weren't any, so we have to assume this is a suicide."

"Don't make any assumptions, Pete," Roni warned her fellow detective.

"Got it, Roni, but it all points to that. Also, we found a BMW in the garage. Judging from the body damage and plates, we think it's the car used to try and run Ricky Gonzalez off the road."

Roni and Trey shared a look that Ricky didn't quite know how to read.

"Can you please get the CSI team to sweep that car for prints and the like? We need to confirm that it was Hernandez who was driving it," Roni said.

"Who else would it have been?" Mariela asked, clearly as puzzled as he by the question.

"I have to trust my gut," Trey said, repeating what he'd said days before about his concerns on the case.

Ricky wasn't about to argue with his brother, even though from everything he could see the case was about as cut and dry as it could be.

When the other detective hung up, they headed to the ME's office.

She was shaking as she viewed her dead ex, but stiffened her spine and identified him. Once she did that, they were free to go and returned to his parents' home. Only once he got there, it occurred to him that there was no reason for Mariela and him to stay there any longer. Whatever threat had existed from Hernandez was over.

That Mariela felt the same way was evident as they climbed the stairs, each step they took feeling the way a death row inmate might on their way to the electric chair.

They paused in the foyer before the two bedrooms, and she said, "I guess I can go home in the morning. Go visit my parents at the assisted living center and let them know what's happening."

"I guess, only..." He took hold of her hand and drew her near. "Stay with me and we can go see your parents together."

She worried her lower lip, obviously hesitant. "That's a big step when we don't know this is real. That it wasn't just because of everything that was happening," she said and pointed to the two of them.

It was a fair enough question and he answered in the only way he could think of.

"Let me prove to you this is real. Tonight, and every other night of our lives together," he said, knowing in his heart that it was what he wanted. That he wanted her in his life forever.

The faint glimmer of a smile broadened and reached up into her eyes, lighting them with joy. "I'd like that, Ricky. I love you."

"I love you, too, Mariela," he said, slipped his hand into hers and led her into his bedroom.

There was no rush, no worry, as they undressed each other and climbed into bed, sealing the promise they'd made each other with their kisses and loving.

As they cuddled close after making love, the rose-colored rays of dawn filtered into the room.

It had been a long and tiring night, but their nightmare was finally over and hope filled Ricky as he thought about his future life together with Mariela.

MARIELA HAD ALWAYS liked rising to see the light of day chasing away the darkness.

She had seen so much of that darkness in her life, but lying there next to Ricky, she knew that her life now would be filled with the light of his love.

Slipping her body over his, she whispered against his lips, "I love you, Ricky. I can't imagine spending the rest of my life without you."

He smiled and rolled, trapping her beneath him, and she experienced a moment of panic, remembering another man and his abuse. But as she met Ricky's clear blue gaze, filled with such light and love, she knew that she'd only ever experience joy in his arms and gave herself over to his loving.

DAYS LATER, IT DIDN'T take a psychologist to see that his brother wasn't accepting the results of the investigations the detectives had conducted into Hernandez's suicide and the BMW they had located in his garage.

"But it wasn't there the first time they checked out his place," Trey argued with his wife as they sat at the dining area table in his parents' home.

"Hernandez could have had it elsewhere. He could have hidden it in one of the warehouses where he kept his construction equipment," Roni said and added, "They didn't see the purple nylon rope the first time either, but it was there in one of the drawers."

"GSR on his gun hand was a little off," Trey said.

"But still consistent with the kind of gunshot residue you'd get with a suicide," Roni advised.

It was like watching a tennis match since for everything that Trey brought up Roni went right back at him with an answer until there were no more questions from Trey.

Roni laid her hand on his arm and squeezed reassuringly. "I trust your gut, Trey. Only this time I think it's a little off. There's no need for us to worry anymore."

With a rough sigh and heave of his broad shoulders, Trey finally agreed. "You're right. It's just that ever since I was shot, I seem to see bogeymen everywhere," he admitted.

Ricky understood. He'd worried that his brother was suffering from PTSD ever since he'd nearly been killed during his last investigation and that could certainly explain how he was feeling. Add to that his leaving the force to join SBS and his upcoming marriage to Roni, things were bound to be off with Trey.

"I can recommend someone you can see—"

"I'm good," Trey said with a flip of his hand, committed to staying the alpha male, but Ricky intended to be there for him and for Mariela, he thought and gazed at her as she sat beside him.

It seemed as good a time as any to share with his brother the news that Mariela and he had shared with his parents the night before.

"I know this might seem sudden, but Mariela and I are going to get married," he said and waited for his brother's admonishments that it was, as Ricky had said, sudden and way too soon.

To his surprise, Trey grinned and clapped his hands with delight. "Congratulations. I was worried at first, but my gut tells me this is right for both of you."

"Wow, really?" he asked as his brother, and Roni rose to hug them.

"Really, *mano*. I know the real thing when I see it," his brother said, filling Ricky with relief.

Everything was right in his world and Mariela's. They had visited her parent to share the news and they'd been happy that Mariela had found someone who loved and respected her. After, they'd talked to his parents about staying until the repairs were finished at his home, and once that was done, they'd move in there and begin the rest of their lives together.

Nothing could be better, he thought, leaned over and kissed Mariela to celebrate the news he'd just shared with Trey and Roni.

HE WATCHED THROUGH the binoculars and wanted to throw up as the family members shared hugs and goodbyes in the courtyard of the family home.

So much happiness and joy while his family had been suffering. While they'd been ignored and the Gonzalez family had become like Miami royalty.

He hated that he'd failed so many times to finish off Ricky, the baby of the family.

The bomb was supposed to have taken him out and maybe some of the others as well, only Ricky's new girl had been too observant.

Next time they might not be so lucky, he thought and drove away.

His family needed him, and he never disappointed family.

* * * * *

Look for the next book in New York Times
bestselling author Caridad Piñeiro's miniseries,
South Beach Security, when
Biscayne Bay Breach *goes on sale*
next month.

And if you missed the first book in the miniseries,
Lost in Little Havana *is available now,*
wherever Harlequin Intrigue books are sold!

Get 4 FREE REWARDS!

We'll send you 2 FREE Books plus 2 FREE Mystery Gifts.

FREE
Value Over
$20

Both the **Harlequin Intrigue**® and **Harlequin**® **Romantic Suspense** series
feature compelling novels filled with heart-racing action-packed romance
that will keep you on the edge of your seat.

Get 4 FREE REWARDS!

We'll send you 2 FREE Books plus 2 FREE Mystery Gifts.

FREE Value Over $20

Both the **Harlequin® Desire** and **Harlequin Presents®** series feature compelling novels filled with passion, sensuality and intriguing scandals.

YES! Please send me 2 FREE novels from the Harlequin Desire or Harlequin Presents series and my 2 FREE gifts (gifts are worth about $10 retail). After receiving them, if I don't wish to receive any more books, I can return the shipping statement marked "cancel." If I don't cancel, I will receive 6 brand-new Harlequin Presents Larger-Print books every month and be billed just $6.30 each in the U.S. or $6.49 each in Canada, a savings of at least 10% off the cover price, or 6 Harlequin Desire books every month and be billed just $5.05 each in the U.S. or $5.74 each in Canada, a savings of at least 12% off the cover price. It's quite a bargain! Shipping and handling is just 50¢ per book in the U.S. and $1.25 per book in Canada.* I understand that accepting the 2 free books and gifts places me under no obligation to buy anything. I can always return a shipment and cancel at any time by calling the number below. The free books and gifts are mine to keep no matter what I decide.

Choose one: ☐ **Harlequin Desire**
(225/326 HDN GRJ7)

☐ **Harlequin Presents Larger-Print**
(176/376 HDN GRJ7)

Name (please print)

Address   Apt. #

City   State/Province   Zip/Postal Code

Email: Please check this box ☐ if you would like to receive newsletters and promotional emails from Harlequin Enterprises ULC and its affiliates. You can unsubscribe anytime.

Mail to the **Harlequin Reader Service:**
IN U.S.A.: P.O. Box 1341, Buffalo, NY 14240-8531
IN CANADA: P.O. Box 603, Fort Erie, Ontario L2A 5X3

Want to try 2 free books from another series! Call 1-800-873-8635 or visit www.ReaderService.com.

HDHP22R3